"Rumor has it I'm the dark brooding type in need of a woman to straighten me out!"

Joshua Staring said as he grinned and watched Lilly's eyes widen. The elevator arrived. Lilly and Joshua stepped inside. When she turned, all the way down the hall, Lilly could see necks craning and the faces of his staff watching them.

Joshua reached around Lilly to push the down button, forcing her into what might look like a cuddling embrace.

"Excuse me," he murmured as the doors closed.

"You did that on purpose," Lilly accused, glaring up at him in astonishment and reproach.

He chuckled, thoroughly enjoying Lilly's outrage. "Gotta give the gossips something to talk about...."

Books by Cheryl Wolverton

Love Inspired

*Hill Creek, Texas

CHERYL WOLVERTON

RITA® Award finalist Cheryl Wolverton has well over a dozen books to her name. Her very popular HILL CREEK, TEXAS series has been a finalist in many contests. Having grown up in Oklahoma, lived in Kentucky, Texas and now Louisiana, Cheryl and her husband of twenty years and their two children, Jeremiah and Christina, consider themselves Oklahomans who have been transplanted to grow and flourish in the South. Readers are always welcome to contact her via: P.O. Box 207, Slaughter, LA 70777, or e-mail at Cheryl@cherylwolverton.com. You can also visit her Web site at www.cherylwolverton.com.

SHELTER
FROM THE
STORM

CHERYL WOLVERTON

Love Inspired.

Published by Steeple Hill Books™

STEEPLE HILL BOOKS

Steeple
Hill™

ISBN 0-373-87205-4

SHELTER FROM THE STORM

Copyright © 2003 by Cheryl Wolverton

All rights reserved. Except for use in any review, the reproduction
or utilization of this work in whole or in part in any form by any
electronic, mechanical or other means, now known or hereafter
invented, including xerography, photocopying and recording, or in
any information storage or retrieval system, is forbidden without
the written permission of the editorial office, Steeple Hill Books,
300 East 42nd Street, New York, NY 10017 U.S.A.

All characters in this book have no existence outside the imagination of
the author and have no relation whatsoever to anyone bearing the same
name or names. They are not even distantly inspired by any individual
known or unknown to the author, and all incidents are pure invention.

This edition published by arrangement with Steeple Hill Books.

® and TM are trademarks of Steeple Hill Books, used under license.
Trademarks indicated with ® are registered in the United States Patent
and Trademark Office, the Canadian Trade Marks Office and in other
countries.

Visit us at www.steeplehill.com

Printed in U.S.A.

...love the Lord your God,
and walk in all His ways, keep His commandments,
and cleave unto Him, and serve Him
with all your heart and with all your soul.

—*Joshua* 22:5

I have to admit this book was fun to write and I fell in love with many of the characters. Part of the reason it was so fun to write was because of two absolutely wonderful teachers at college: Dr. Isaac Belonga and Dr. Fernando Figueroa. Their classes were fun and energizing, and I came home full of fresh ideas and wanting to write and express myself. What a refreshing way to write!

Also, thank you to Steve, Christina and Jeremiah who have all fallen into the routine of a writing wife/mother. They're the greatest!

And finally to my mom, Helen Weaver. I love you, Mom.

Prologue

Lilly Hammond thinks she's smart. She's moved again. She's no longer here in Philadelphia. Of course, she was never really meant to be a secretarial assistant at that lawyer's office. She evidently realized that when the office burned down and the lawyer was caught in the fire. I hadn't expected her to flee that fast, however.

Still, her flight won't stop me. It didn't stop me in the past when she found Jesus and insisted she could no longer be a part of our group—be a part of me. I let her try her little strategies. I let her have her time to think about the consequences of leaving us, but it's time to put an end to that.

It's time to take command of this cat-and-mouse game. It's time I remind her of just who is in control.

I'm coming Lilly.

Are you ready?

Chapter One

The unusual night fog had rolled into the Pride, Louisiana, area. Joshua Staring carefully maneuvered his car through the eerie patches of white that grew thicker the closer he got to the warehouse district on Choctaw in Baton Rouge where his offices were located.

It was late at night, later than most people were out on the road. It was just after midnight, but Joshua didn't sleep much, and liked to go in to the office late at night to catch up on work.

The night lent a feeling of solitude to his drive, reminding him of how much he preferred the quiet—and loneliness.

His security business was booming and during the day he had constant appointments with corporations and homeowners who wanted top-notch security in the tristate area. Large and small they all came to Staring Security, hoping to find someone who could protect them from the outside, the enemy, the sick depraved underworld who lurked just out of sight waiting for their chance to rob, rape and ravage the homes of the people wanting security.

Many of his clients were corporations and businesses that were targets of thieves or industrial spies. That's where the money was.

Joshua recommended simple security systems to most of his clients, but many of them didn't want inexpensive systems. They wanted state-of-the-art security, the best money could buy. These clients were convinced that the destruction they read in the daily news would certainly touch their lives if they didn't have the best security available.

Formerly an FBI agent, Joshua could see why people felt the way they did.

He couldn't fault the average citizen for wanting their houses and families secured against crime and mayhem. Bad things did happen.

People did break in and did kill other people who were innocents and not involved in any way in the dark side of the world. People who shouldn't be involved, who should have been protected and safe were attacked and killed. People like Carrie and Andy.

Bitterly, Joshua pushed the old memories aside, forcing himself to think in the here and now. Solitude was what he wanted and would get—peace and quiet and solitude to work.

Work was his escape. Work filled everything that had been left empty by the loss. It, for a short time, erased the guilt and pain that constantly haunted him.

It helped him to forget what God had allowed to happen.

Crossing the railroad tracks, he turned onto the road where his company was located and quickly punched in the security code to enter the employee parking area.

The heat and humidity hung heavy in the air, only cooling enough to increase the nasty fog that dimmed anyone's ability to drive safely in the haze. He really shouldn't be out in it, but needed the work, the escape from the night.

As he entered the lot he noted another car in the parking area.

His executive secretary.

What would Lilly be doing here this late? She rarely stayed past eight. She was a workaholic like he was, he knew, having often caught her at work in the evenings. But this late at night?

Maybe the fog had trapped her here, preventing her from driving home.

He didn't know much about his secretary. She was the quiet sort, getting her job done with minimal conversation. She was thirty-two and had never been married. She'd left her last job, she said, because she wanted a new life in a big city. Originally from a small town in the southwest, she'd moved here and started from scratch.

He'd actually met her through a temporary agency when he needed someone to fill in for his secretary who had taken maternity leave. He'd found her work excellent. Things had never run more smoothly and he never noticed her there.

Just what he wanted—a quiet individual who knew her place, didn't bother him and worked miracles. She was the perfect secretary for him.

When he realized Mary, his old secretary, wasn't coming back, he'd offered Lilly the job full-time.

She'd been working for him for three months now.

He hadn't regretted it at all.

Shoving his car door open he swung his legs out and stood. Pausing to rub his sore right knee, he thought the weather must be changing. His knee only bothered him this much in the pressure changes that came before a storm.

Grabbing his walking stick, he stood and then locked the door behind him. Clicking on the security system, he pocketed his keys and headed toward the door of Staring Security.

Nodding to the security officer in the front, he passed by without a word.

At the elevator, he inserted his card and took the elevator to the fourth floor where his office was located.

The business had grown, with the first floor being entirely devoted to purchasing and administration. The second floor contained much of the day-to-day working staff that kept the houses and businesses secure. On the third floor were managers' offices. Fourth floor housed the offices for the company's executives: his main security officer, Angelina Harding; computer security, Davie Warren; home security, Matt Martin; and corporate security, Todd Ashcroft.

Stepping out of the elevator he quietly made his way past the empty secretarial desks that handled overflow from the executive secretaries. Gilded mirrors dotted the hallway along with yellow-and-orange floral arrangements on the small tables.

Chairs near each reception area, dark-brown and gold, the material thick and comfy, waited to be filled each day with new people seeking an inspection of their property and evaluation of their security needs.

Approaching the end of the long hall he noted the receptionist's desk was also empty, but heard the soft sounds of a radio from inside his secretary's office.

The door was open and he crossed the entrance, only to stop short as he noted someone bent over the desk going through the credenza.

Lilly was dressed in blue jeans and a soft blue top with a fuzzy blue-and-silver sweater. It certainly wasn't the type of outfit he was used to seeing his secretary in. Lilly normally wore dark-blue suits, with her hair pulled up and oversize glasses perched on her nose.

Tonight, however, her hair was down. Golden highlights touched the dark-brown hair. Natural, he thought, watching as the shoulder-length hair brushed over her shoulder as she pulled another file out and stuck it under her arm. He couldn't have said before tonight what color hair she had. Now he would never forget. The overhead lights caught the gold and made it glow.

He wondered where her glasses were.

Feeling like a voyeur he shifted slightly then went forward, crossing the plush carpet. He'd hoped she'd realize someone else was in the room. It didn't work, though, as the carpet muffled the sound of his cane as well as his footsteps. He was now within arm's length of her. Soon she would figure out he was here and they both were going to be embarrassed. He knew Lilly wouldn't like the fact that someone had managed to sneak up on her. And he also felt uncomfortable. Forty years old and feeling unsettled in the presence of a woman who didn't even know he was there? He could see the humor in the situation, and he hoped his secretary would, too. She still riffled through the files, oblivious to him.

Pushing aside the uncomfortable feelings, he smiled sardonically, impressed that he had actually sneaked up on this sharp-eyed guard dog. Softly, so as not to startle her, he said, "Ms. Hammond."

It didn't work. And boy was he *not* ready for her response.

Her scream split the quiet office. Terror flashed in her eyes as she turned, folders in hand, swinging out at him.

As quick as he used to be, he found he'd lost that edge because of his disabling injury. Unable to get out of her way, he tried to brace himself as she slammed into him. It did no good. He went flying backward—his walking stick one way, folders from her hands the other.

With a thud he fell hard onto the mauve carpet. Lilly Hammond came to rest, sprawled backward over her desk, clearing it as she did.

Pain ricocheted from his knee outward in all directions—to his foot, up his thigh.

He closed his eyes and gritted his teeth as wave after wave of agony shot through him.

"Oh, dear! Mr. Staring! I'm—I'm so sorry. I didn't know anyone else was here. Let me help you. Are you okay?"

The husky alto voice drew closer.

Opening his eyes he saw her leaning over him. The terror was gone from her gaze, but she was babbling now—a sure sign of adrenaline rush.

"I didn't mean to scare you," he said through his still-gritted teeth.

The pain was abating. It would take a moment, but it would be bearable soon.

As he lay there attempting to regain control, he noticed Lilly's eyes were a sapphire blue. And they were filled with worry.

She bit her lip and reached out, tentatively touching his shoulder. She looked ready to cry.

"My walking stick," he said simply, giving

her a way to release some of that pent-up energy.

He'd seen it many times in the people he had worked with. He'd learned through the years that it behooved him to help them work the adrenaline out of their system.

Lilly scrambled to her feet and rushed over to where his cane lay. She snatched it up and brought it back to him.

His pain was now under control and he took the stick from her. Shifting, he lifted himself up and got the black ivory-headed rod under his weight and stood.

Lilly stepped back and then, her nervousness propelling her, she started gathering files. "I had no idea—I mean—no one was here when I showed up—"

"What *are* you doing here this late?" he asked mildly.

She stopped gathering the folders and stood, clutching the ones she had in her hands to her chest. "I—was—well, there's a hurricane coming and I knew that might interrupt power—"

Hurricane? His mind left Lilly and her explanation as he turned and walked past her desk to his office door. Shoving it open, he hurried inside.

His office was spacious, everything he might need there including a small refrigerator, microwave, shower—all hidden from view. But most of all, he had his televisions. Some were closed-circuit monitors for the security of the building but one was dedicated to satellite TV.

Going to his desk he pulled open the top left drawer and grabbed a remote. Inside the drawer he hit a button and an area of his bookshelves slid open to reveal the televisions. Pointing the remote, he turned on one of the TVs and flipped it to a weather channel.

Lilly had followed him, folders still clutched to her chest. "I realized, you see, that hurricanes sometimes cause power interruptions. That would be an ideal time for looting...."

She trailed off.

He heard her but concentrated his attention on the weather broadcast. "I hadn't watched any TV today and had no idea we had bad weather coming our way."

The report came on TV and he found himself relaxing as the forecaster talked. "Where are you from, Ms. Hammond?"

Slowly he lowered himself to his chair and propped his leg up on the footstool underneath his desk that he used when his knee bothered him.

Lilly blinked, those deep-blue eyes going wide at the question. He had never noticed how beautiful they were before. Her glasses certainly hid a lot.

"Lawton, Oklahoma."

He nodded. "Have you ever been in a hurricane?"

Slowly she shook her head. "This is the first one since I've been down here."

A small smile played about his lips. He was a loner and didn't deal with people except in a business setting. Even then, his employees set up most of the appointments and Joshua didn't get involved until the third appointment.

By then everything was done, fees paid, the only thing left was the implementation of the security issues.

Since he didn't usually deal with people who weren't from the area, he tended to forget what he took for normal was strange to people not from the Gulf Coast or Louisiana.

Patiently he nodded to a chair. "Have a seat, Ms. Hammond."

Nervously she glanced back at her office where he could still see scattered folders. "It's after midnight, so there's no hurry to clean up. No one's going to know what happened. Have a seat."

Surprised when she blushed, he had to admit this side of his secretary caught his interest.

Once she was seated he motioned to the TV. "The tropical depression is still in the Atlantic."

She nodded. "They said it was going to hit here."

He shook his head. "It'll be a good week or so before it gets here, if it continues on its present course." Studying the screen again and what was being said, he added, "The trajectory does make it look like it's coming right into the Gulf. However, we're talking a week at least. In that time the upper-level winds could change direction, the jet stream could shift and push it on up the eastern seaboard. There are too many possibilities to count right now. And if it does enter the gulf, Texas and Alabama could be hit as well. And if it hits Louisiana, according to how strong the depression develops, it might not even make it to Baton Rouge except for some rain."

Now his secretary was really red. Her eyes slid away to one side. "I'm so sorry. I was at home and saw this and wanted to have everything ready in case you came in tomorrow and wanted information on the most likely break-in areas and—"

"Whoa," he said.

Rubbing his neck he had to wonder if she saw him the way he was seeing himself. "I'm not that demanding, Lilly."

At her incredulous expression he shifted, perturbed.

She swallowed and her face went neutral, no smile or frown, simple professionalism displayed for him to see. "Of course not, Mr. Staring. You're just efficient. You like things to run smoothly and that's my job—to see things run smoothly for you."

He'd wanted to be alone in his office to work with no one to bother him. He'd wanted to be busy enough to keep his mind off the past. But here he was with his secretary. Or someone impersonating the hard-nosed, efficient bulldog that usually took care of sifting out the world for him and making sure he got whatever he needed. He found for the first time in a long time he was actually enjoying a moment with someone of the opposite sex. Not only a member of the opposite sex—his secretary. Disconcerting, to say the least.

Perhaps it was the way he'd surprised her that had let down both of their guards, or the fact she'd knocked him flat on his back.

Maybe the pain in his knee had caused him to forget the shell he erected to keep everyone away.

On the other hand, maybe it was the way this woman was dressed, the soft vulnerable look, the look of terror when he'd surprised her that awakened old feelings of protection and curiosity. Whatever it was, he knew from their brief conversation tonight that Lilly Hammond had managed to sneak under his shell and it was going to take a while to get her back out.

But first, he wanted to find out more about that look of fear he'd seen in her eyes.

Joshua Staring knew people. And Lilly was a person who was hiding something, a secret he was going to uncover.

Chapter Two

Lilly was mortified to be caught at Staring Security in the middle of the night. Especially by her boss.

She hadn't been able to sleep. Two hang-up calls this evening had rattled her and made old fears rise up in her, fears from the past, from her former life before she'd become a Christian.

The idea that someone might have found out once again where she was danced in her mind, refusing to give her a rest. When she'd heard her name, whispered so closely to her and her mind had still been on her past—well, suffice to say, that had been her undoing.

"I'll tell you what, if you promise to have those files on my desk in a week if I need them, then I promise not to be upset if the storm hits earlier than that."

It took a moment for her to realize what he meant. She felt herself flushing again.

Mr. Staring was a good man to work for, competent, always on the job, never noticing her or what she did as long as she kept things in order and ready for him.

It had been so easy to slip into the job. All she had to do was listen and watch—something she was good at—to figure out what he was going to want and when he would need it. And as she did that, she'd found he never noticed more than the fact she worked there.

Of course, the other women in the company wondered how a temporary worker had snagged such a cushy position. Every one of them would have given their eyeteeth to work for the handsome, single CEO.

Lilly wondered if maybe that's why she got the job. Though she found him terribly good-looking, with his dark eyes and dark hair, she wasn't interested in the least.

As a new Christian she had been so busy healing from the past, slowly learning how to face the world again and start living that she didn't have *time* for a man. Of course, the past was gone and she wanted it to stay that way. So, she wasn't sure she could afford to have anything to do with a man, especially someone in Mr. Staring's area of expertise.

This job was a blessing and a curse. She felt much safer here with the guards and security-conscious people than she did anywhere else. However, it could be a curse if her boss were to get curious about her. He was the type who could find out anything he wanted. She hadn't needed to worry about the last—until now, she thought, seeing that look of musing on his face as he stared at her. *God help keep me safe and unknown,* she silently prayed.

"Ms. Hammond?"

Realizing she'd been gazing at him blankly, she said, "I'm sorry. Of course, Mr. Staring. That'll be fine. I'll make sure to have a list ready if the storm does approach. And I'll brush up on hurricanes. I should have done that when I first moved here."

She offered him a polite smile.

He returned her smile and Lilly saw why women wanted to be around him. All of a sudden, Lilly found she had difficulty swallowing. He was really a handsome man, she realized.

"I guess I should be going."

Steepling his fingers in front of him, Joshua Staring shook his head. "The fog is really too thick to drive in. There's a fog advisory out." Slowly he pointed a finger at the TV.

She glanced around and noted there was indeed an advisory flashing on the screen.

Turning back to face him, she straightened the folders in her lap. "I'm not usually up here this late," she murmured into the silence.

It was always the silence that got to her. She hated to be in a room with the focus on her.

"I didn't think you were."

"I hope it's not a problem," she added.

He smiled. "If it had been a problem, Ms. Hammond, Angelina would have notified me."

She nodded, her gaze still on the folders.

When she didn't say anything else, Joshua Staring whispered, "So what really brought you up here tonight, Lilly Hammond?"

Her gaze jerked to his in stunned surprised.

His fingers still steepled in front of him, his expression inscrutable, he stared at her.

"I—I really did want to get the papers ready."

Releasing his pose, he waved a hand. "I believe that. That's not what I meant."

"Oh." Lilly blinked.

Silence fell.

He couldn't know about the calls, could he?

The silence stretched.

Finally he sighed. "I'll tell you what. You're a trusted employee here, Ms. Hammond. If you need my help, or need someone to talk to about anything, you can come to me. Okay?"

Relieved he wasn't going to pursue the cause of her disquiet, she nodded. "Thank you, Mr. Staring."

He smiled slightly. "Call me Joshua after hours. You are, after all, my personal secretary."

She stiffened.

He sighed. "That didn't sound very good, did it? I simply meant we work together a lot so it's okay to be on more familiar terms after…" He shook his head.

"I know what you mean," Lilly said finally, surprised to actually see her boss embarrassed. "And I understand that wasn't a come-on."

He smiled. "No. You'd definitely know a come-on from me if I tried it."

Now that, she thought, was a come-on— whether he realized it or not. That quirky smile, flashing eyes and deepening voice as he'd said that, even if he was joking, had just lit a fire in the pit of her stomach.

She swallowed again.

"I should get my desk picked up so when the guard makes his rounds he doesn't think World War Three has broken out. And then, when the fog clears, I'll leave."

He nodded. "Let me help you."

He went to move his leg and winced.

"Are you okay?" Lilly asked, standing in concern.

He rubbed his knee. "Yeah. An old injury that flares up occasionally."

She nodded, wanting to help him but knowing better than to cross that line. "How did it happen?" she asked, thinking that an innocent enough question.

Evidently it wasn't as his face darkened.

"If you don't want to answer—" she began, only to be cut off.

"It's no secret. I used to be a marshal. One particular case...went bad. I was shot in the knee. It effectively ended my career."

Seeing the shadows in his eyes, Lilly thought that injury must still haunt him. How dark he looked as he said that, how deeply disturbed.

"It bothers me when the weather is changing, or if I move suddenly."

"Like falling down," Lilly muttered apologetically.

He chuckled. "Yeah. That could do it, too."

She thought that in the few months she'd been here this was the first time she'd heard him laugh. She'd seen more smiles and learned more about her boss in the last ten minutes than she had the entire time she'd been working for him.

He must be really different when he was off work, she thought as she stopped by her desk.

Going down to her knees she started picking up paper clips, folders, pens and such and handing them up to Joshua as he stood by the desk to assist her.

"Has your business always been this busy?" she asked as she passed him several folders.

"Not at first. It took time. I moved here to Baton Rouge to find some friends to help me run it. We put in a lot of footwork to get it up and going. But when our reputation for fast service, good prices and top-of-the-line technology got around and before we knew it, we'd outgrown our little storefront building and I was looking for more help. It's been five years now and the size has doubled many times over."

"I'm impressed," Lilly said and stood. Moving around Joshua, she started straightening her desk. "They say it takes five years for a business to be made or broken."

"Did you notice the one-dollar bill on my wall?"

She nodded. Turning to the credenza she started putting folders back into it. "That was your first earning dollar?"

"It sure was. We joke about it now, that if the business ever goes bust, we're going to have to split it five ways."

Glancing over her shoulder at Mr. Staring

she asked curiously, "With the other four people on this floor, you mean?"

He nodded.

Inquisitively she asked, "They started the business with you?"

"Not exactly. Actually, they're all former colleagues of mine. They each put in some money to help me get started when I decided to start my own business."

"And they all ended up here?"

He nodded. "We make a good team."

Lilly pondered that as she finished her filing. Closing the credenza she finally turned to face the man before her. Nearly six foot five she felt short standing next to him, which was a feat since she was five foot ten. But it felt nice to stand beside a man who was so much taller. It felt nice and safe. She wondered if Joshua Staring realized he exuded a field of reassurance and security.

"You sure do make a good team," she reassured. Business wouldn't be booming if they didn't make such a good team, she thought. "I should go downstairs and wait for the fog to clear."

She wasn't sure but she thought she saw a flicker of disappointment in Joshua's eyes at her statement.

"Be careful driving home."

She nodded and grabbed her purse—just as her telephone rang.

Lilly jumped like she'd been poked with a hot iron.

"Easy," Joshua said, his large hand coming down on her shoulder. The warmth of his touch went a long way to calming her fears.

"Expecting a call?" he asked and she wanted to glare at him. Obviously, from her reaction, he knew she wasn't expecting a call— at least one that she wanted to take.

She shrugged. "Not really." She wasn't going to admit her heart rate had doubled at that ring and that she was beginning to sweat.

When she didn't move to pick it up, he asked, "Are you going to answer it?"

All night as she'd been here working, she had convinced herself that the calls she'd gotten at her house were wrong numbers or telemarketers. That happened a lot. The problem was, when a person was on the run, any call that wasn't expected held the portent for doom or despair.

Just like this call here. If she'd only had those calls at home, then she might believe this call was a mistake. But who would be calling her at the office this late at night?

Despite her attempt at bravado she shook her head.

And that was that. She could act as brave as she wanted, but the fear that they had found her... No. She wasn't answering the telephone.

Joshua snagged the receiver. "Staring—"

She gripped his arm, her face draining of color. "No!" she hissed.

"—Security."

She sucked in a breath and waited.

"Ah, Angelina," he said and gave Lilly an odd look.

Oh, heavens! She nearly collapsed in relief. It was only Joshua's security specialist on the line. Then she realized she'd just made a fool of herself in front of her boss! She backed away to leave, but Joshua held up a hand. "Hold on, Angelina."

Lowering the phone Joshua gave Lilly a

stern look. "I expect you here first thing in the morning. If you run, which is exactly what the look on your face indicates you might do, I'll hunt you down."

She opened her mouth to object, to say she wasn't going to run. But in fact, that had been her exact thought. Joshua was way too good at reading people...and her, she realized. That didn't bode well at all.

"I'm here to listen, Ms. Hammond—*Lilly,*" he emphasized her first name, "if you need me. Okay?"

Shaking her head in disbelief she whispered, "Okay."

He gave her a smile of compassion. "If you'd rather talk now—"

"No!"

He sighed. "Okay, go home. Try to sleep on it. I'll see you in the morning." Reaching for a piece of paper on her desk, he pulled out a pen and wrote down his home phone number. "Keep this with you."

She accepted the paper with conflicting emotions. Nodding, not saying another word, she headed for the elevator.

What was she going to do? Three months here and things had been great. And now in one night she'd totally blown everything.

There was only one thing to do.

Run.

Chapter Three

"Let me go into my office. Hold on."

Heading into his office he closed the door and turned on the speakerphone. "I'm back."

"So what was that about?" Angelina asked, her voice coming over the speaker clearly.

Joshua sat down at his desk and carefully propped his leg up. "My secretary was here."

"Oh re-e-eally?"

The way she said that, so drawn out and full of innuendo, made him grimace. "It's not like that."

"Oh, come on, Joshua. No one would blame you if it was."

He scowled. "Angie, darling, you might be a good friend, but butt out."

She chuckled.

"So why are you calling me in the middle of the night on my secretary's line?"

"Just checking up on you. And you didn't answer your private line."

"I was in my secretary's office."

"Yeah, Charles told me she was there when I called downstairs."

"Well, I hope you know by calling on her line, you scared the soup out of her."

"Soup?" She chuckled. "Never have learned to curse right and for that I have to say I'm impressed."

He rolled his eyes. The people at the office had always given him a hard time over his expressions. They all knew he was a Christian and had chosen not to swear—though occasionally words did slip out, more and more of late—which was probably why Angie was teasing him.

One by one, however, his friends had found Jesus as their savior—most of them at least. Angie was one of the exceptions.

"So tell me, why would my call scare her?"

Joshua, who had been rubbing his knee, paused. "I don't know. I think she was expecting someone she didn't want to talk to."

"At this time of night?"

He shrugged then said, "Again, I'm not sure. I told her I wanted to talk to her in the morning about it."

"Taking a personal interest in your secretary's problems?"

"Her name is Lilly Hammond," he replied lightly.

"Taking a personal interest in Lilly's problems?"

"Who says she has any problems?" Joshua retorted.

"You forget I can read you like a book, as can Todd, Matt and Davie. Like a book, Josh. It's in your nature. You care. And I for one am glad to see you taking a personal interest in someone again—even if it is your secretary."

Joshua scowled. "You didn't call me up to lecture me about my secretary."

"No, I didn't. I was having trouble sleeping and noted there's a disturbance headed toward the gulf."

"I know." Disgusted, he shifted in his chair.

"And if you're suggesting that we should prepare for something—"

"Of course not," Angelina interrupted. "It's way too early. But it did get me to thinking. We've been having trouble with our backup generator. Since it is getting to that season we might want to look into purchasing a new one."

He nodded. "That's a good idea. Put that down for us to discuss in the meeting tomorrow. In the meantime we can borrow the one from the bunker until we can purchase a new one."

"Sounds good. There's something else."

"Yes?" he asked, knowing that couldn't have been the only reason for her to call.

"I have a…problem…I need to take care of. I won't be able to make it in tomorrow. Can you have Todd present my notes at the meeting if I fax them to his desk?"

"Sure thing. And why aren't you calling Todd about this?"

"He's not home."

Joshua let out a loud sigh. "Is anyone home tonight?"

"I am," Angelina quipped.

He nodded. "Okay. We've got you covered. Is it anything you need help with?" he asked, old ties and memories of the many times they'd all shared together fresh in his mind.

She hesitated, her voice dropping a bit, indicating she was worried about something. "No. It'll be fine."

"Women," Joshua muttered.

"Hey, men are just as stubborn."

He shook his head. "Not by a long shot. Take care and be careful."

"I sure will. And you get some sleep."

He clicked off the speakerphone.

Sleep.

Did he ever get sleep anymore?

Actually, he realized, he had come in to do work and get rid of some of his restless energy, to forget some of the past. He realized that most of that restlessness was gone. He felt more relaxed than he had in a while.

Except for one small thing.

Lilly Hammond.

What was she hiding?

Turning to the computer on his work desk, he turned it on. He was eager for that chat with her tomorrow.

Chapter Four

❧

"Was there anything else that needed discussing today?" Joshua asked and started to stand.

Matt shoved his papers to the side. "Where's Angelina?"

They'd been here since 7:00 a.m. and it was now eight-thirty. Though Joshua really wanted to dismiss the meeting, he sat back down with a sigh. He looked around the table at his staff.

Matt was the ultimate protector, although he didn't look the part. He looked more like a street thug: long hair pulled back in a neat ponytail, loose jeans, matching jacket, white

T-shirt and old tennis shoes. He wore a base-ball cap when he wasn't inside the building.

His appearance disguised the sharp intelligence that came with being a former FBI agent. He'd been used to working undercover until only two years ago. Now he used his savvy to direct the home security unit.

"I'd sorta like to know that, too," Todd added. He, in contrast to Matt, wore a charcoal-gray suit and conservative dark tie. Unlike Joshua, Todd enjoyed his desk job—the reason he worked so well with corporations. Of course, his job with the agency had been planning strategies. He had great instincts when it came to finding the security weakness of an individual or corporation.

Glancing at Davie, the computer geek of the group, Joshua asked, "Are you going to question me, too?"

The youngest of them, Davie, shoved the glasses up on his nose. His hair looked unkempt and his gaze distracted as he shrugged. "Nah. She's in Australia."

Joshua blinked.

"Australia?" Matt barked.

"And she didn't invite us," Todd added lazily.

Joshua didn't ask Davie how he knew where Angelina was. Angelina hadn't even told him where she was going. Davie just had a way of always knowing things.

Before this meeting could get any more out of hand, Joshua explained, "She had some personal business to take care of and if she needs us I'm sure she'll call."

Matt snorted.

Todd gave that slow smile of his that drove most ladies crazy while Davie only shrugged again. Though he acted distracted and didn't seem to be on top of what was going on, Joshua speculated that Davie was probably the only one who really knew what Angelina was up to. He knew more about computers than any of them, his job in intelligence requiring that skill of him and he used his laptop in ways that had Joshua simply shaking his head with amazement.

The buzzer on his desk sounded.

"Yes?" Joshua asked into the intercom.

"Your secretary is here, Mr. Staring." Rita,

the secretary who was currently working the reception desk outside of Lilly's office, notified him.

All three men quieted. Matt looked on with unchecked curiosity while Todd was a bit more circumspect. Davie, on the other hand, leaned forward and typed a few words on the computer screen in front of him. He always brought his laptop to staff meetings; Todd usually brought a legal pad and Matt never wrote anything down.

This was one of the problems with the team setup, Joshua mused. There were very few secrets in this operation. If he didn't cut them off now, they would start an entire new round of questions. For instance, why was Joshua so interested in his secretary's arrival? Seeing Davie clicking away on the keyboard, he realized Davie was probably making notes to check out later.

He scowled, "Don't even think about it, Davie." Rubbing his knee, he adjusted his leg so he could stand and shoved his chair under the table. "I need to talk to her privately." The others took his words as a dismissal. They stood as well.

Joshua shrugged. At Matt's inscrutable look, he sighed. He wasn't going to get out of this without some sort of explanation. "I think she's running. We had a talk last night and I wasn't sure she was going to show up today."

"Want me to check her out?" Davie asked.

"Not yet," Joshua said.

"I'll be glad to have a chat with her," Todd offered.

Again, Joshua shook his head.

"I'll keep an eye on her," Matt stated and then turned. "Later," he called over his shoulder as he headed toward the door. *Later* was Matt's way of saying goodbye.

What a way to start the day and what poor timing. Joshua was certain that because that phone message from Rita had come at precisely the *wrong* time, all three men would be watching Lilly like a hawk for the next week or two.

It was the nature of their business to be suspicious.

Poor Lilly.

Thank heavens Angelina wasn't here. She would just go ahead and question Lilly outright.

"Let me know if any more problems crop up," Joshua said to Todd and Davie, referring to a recurring security glitch that they had discussed earlier during the meeting.

Without waiting for a reply he walked to the door, opened it and nodded as the men left.

Then he leaned against the doorjamb, crossed one leg in front of the other, slipped his hands into his dark-gray pants, and waited for Lilly, who was slipping her purse into her bottom desk drawer, to look up at him.

She knew he was there.

He could tell in the way she stiffened.

He never noticed her being uncomfortable with his presence before.

More than likely it was because she'd debated running but remembered his warning of the night before.

He'd been in the business too long not to have noticed the signs.

Boy did she look good today.

Light-gray pants, pink top, her hair pulled up. She looked very un-Lilly again. Where was her dark-blue suit?

"Nice outfit," he said when she turned to face him.

She had just opened her mouth to say something.

At his comment, she snapped it shut.

He smiled.

"Come on in," he invited and turned so she could slip past him.

She hesitated, shifted and then reached for a pad and pencil and hurried into his office.

Her oversize glasses were back in place, attempting to hide the beauty of her blue eyes.

He remembered the color from last night. No amount of covering would block that memory, he thought as he turned and followed her into his office.

Oh, yeah, all the signs were there. She'd started to run.

He went to his desk and sat down in the large leather chair and leaned back. Steepling his fingers, he studied her. "You look tired, Lilly."

She had just seated herself and flipped open her notepad. She paused.

Finally her gaze met his and she said, honestly and forthrightly, "I started to leave."

He nodded. "I'm not surprised."

Her eyes reflected the scowl she kept from her face. She didn't like the fact that he seemed to be able to read her so easily.

"I like privacy," she finally admitted.

"So you went to work for a security firm?"

She shrugged, her gaze sliding away. "It was a job."

He nodded. "Fair enough."

She fidgeted.

He let her squirm for a moment before finally coming to the point. "Your last boss was killed in a fire."

Her gaze shot to his. Lines creased both sides of her mouth as she froze. It was barely noticeable in the way her shoulders squared and the way she withdrew, but there he had it. The truth in her reaction to his stunning discovery.

"You checked up on me." Her voice came out barely above a whisper. Her brain worked behind those eyes. She most assuredly wanted to run now, but he wasn't planning to let her.

"Lilly Hammond. Born in Lawton, Oklahoma, but living in Philadelphia before coming here. The week you left there was a fire. The question is, did you leave before or after the fire?''

That stubborn chin of hers lifted slightly. It was a last-ditch effort to retain her composure.

Unfortunately for Joshua, he felt something he rarely experienced for a person he was interrogating—he felt sympathy.

It was a strange feeling to come at this time. He had her pinned with the truth, yet, seeing the look in her eyes... He didn't want to question her further. Instead, he had the craziest urge to reach out and just hold her and let her cry it out. He hadn't done that in a long time. He could remember the last time, in fact. And it made him acutely uncomfortable.

Instead of acting on his desire to comfort, he shifted slightly in his seat so he could cross his legs and concentrated on staying seated while he spoke. ''It's okay, Lilly. I don't think you had anything to do with the fire.'' Though he'd tried to stay objective, his voice lowered with concern. ''You're running from something, that's obvious.''

''My fiancé,'' she whispered.

Brought up short, Joshua asked, ''Excuse me?''

Obviously not noting his stunned response, Lilly said, "It wasn't really public knowledge, but the man who died had asked me to marry him."

"You were engaged?" He would not have guessed that, looking at her. She didn't show signs of such a loss. He didn't like that she had been engaged either. Scowling, he waited for her to continue.

Lilly hesitated then shook her head. "Not exactly. He had asked me. I had thought about saying yes." Her gaze slid away.

"But instead you ran."

She nodded. "I heard about the fire the next day when I tried to call and couldn't get hold of him. I was going to come back and talk to him, and well…"

"But…?" Joshua asked. He didn't know why the thought of her being involved with someone bothered him so much.

Again she shook her head. "I wasn't ready for marriage. I'd just come out of a rough relationship. I guess he thought by marrying me he could pro—"

Her eyes widened and she stopped talking in the middle of the word.

"Pro? Protect you?"

She didn't answer.

She didn't have to. He could read it in her gaze. He relaxed. It had been a proposal of convenience. She hadn't loved him and the lawyer hadn't loved her.

She simply shrugged. "Then this job came open and I needed something that would keep me busy." Sighing, she confessed, "I only wanted to put the past in the past."

Joshua thought about that. He thought about her fear when the phone rang last night. He didn't like the picture that was forming in his mind, but he knew this woman wasn't going to tell him everything right now.

That bothered him. Yet he understood. Just like Carrie and Andy, a mother and child he'd been protecting years ago, this woman thought she could handle it on her own. She'd been injured one too many times to trust someone.

He wasn't even sure why he cared, except that he did. Lilly had caught his attention last night and man, was he finding it hard to let go.

He leaned back. "I'm glad you came to work today, Lilly."

She shifted, obviously wanting to say something but not sure about what type of privilege she could take with him. He smiled. "What's on your mind?"

"I don't want to leave. Last night and even this morning I tried but..."

He waited.

She clasped her hands in front of her, twisting them above the pen and pad in her lap. He wondered if she had any idea that her body language clearly demonstrated her inner turmoil.

"But...?" he prodded.

"I like this job. I like it here. I've found somewhere that I... Well, that's safe."

"You don't have to leave, Lilly."

She hesitated before lifting her gaze to meet his. A look of vulnerability filled that gaze, reaching out and wrapping around his heart, dragging him into her world and holding him there. "I wish I could confide some of this, but...it's too soon—I didn't expect anyone to find out anything and yet...well...I just can't, sir."

He shook his head. "It's fine, Lilly. And you don't have to tell me anything, for now."

He wanted to get up, go around the desk and take her hand in his and squeeze. He wanted to let her know he cared. Instead, he did his best to will his feelings into his voice as he said, "The team knows there's a problem. That's enough to make sure you're safe."

The gratitude that filled her eyes caused a lump in his chest, making him feel special. Embarrassing, but true. He wasn't certain but he also thought, behind those glasses, he saw tears.

Curse her for hiding those eyes of hers, he thought ruefully, wishing he had some sort of protection right now from the emotions she was making him feel.

"Thank you."

Deciding they'd had enough "touchy-feely" for one day—he certainly didn't want to deal with tears—he turned his attention to business. "Angelina called last night," he said. "She mentioned that our generator is shot and we should shop around for a new one. We'll probably bring the one from the bunker up here."

He knew she understood the bunker to mean the house he had in Pride. The entire team called it the bunker because it always seemed when there was a problem, that was where they hunkered down to handle it.

Lilly started writing notes, purely professional, closing off all emotion as she wrote.

Joshua admired her for that—a lot. Standing, he grabbed his cane, walked across to the windows and looked out over Baton Rouge noting that the smog over the thirty-two-story state capital building wasn't too bad today. Such a contrast to Pride, a country town about thirty minutes away. Right now it was lush, green and very tropical looking as the summer plants were all in bloom. Lilly needed to experience the country. Did she live in Baton Rouge or one of the smaller surrounding towns? He didn't know where she lived, he realized.

Forcing himself to turn and face his secretary he said, "We'll also need to make sure we are stocked up on emergency supplies—flashlights, batteries, blankets, first-aid kits, water, et cetera. Make a note to have someone look into that. Also ask Davie to find out just where Angelina is and have her call me when she gets a chance?"

"Of course, Mr.—"

He lifted an eyebrow in amusement.

"Joshua," she amended.

He chuckled. "Thanks."

"Is that all?" she asked, her posture relaxing as a small smile danced about the corners of her mouth.

He nodded.

She stood and went to the door. When she pulled it open, she halted, surprised.

Matt stood just outside.

Startled for only a moment, Lilly moved past him with a murmured good-morning. As she went to her desk, Matt walked up to Joshua's office doorway.

Joshua should have known dismissing his partners wouldn't end their curiosity about the situation between Lilly and himself. More than likely, Matt would simply have gone to his office to do whatever he needed to do to check up on Lilly and would return to grill Joshua later.

He was the most obstinate of the group.

"And hold my calls. It looks like I'm going to be in another meeting."

Lilly nodded. "Yes, sir."

Lifting an eyebrow, Joshua slipped his hands into his pocket. "So, what's up, Matt?"

Matt came into the office and closed the door behind him with an easygoing nudge. "I thought I'd ask the same of you, Josh."

Joshua simply stared.

Matt motioned to the other office with his head.

Letting out an exasperated breath, Joshua shifted his walking stick and moved over to a sofa and dropped down onto it. Absently rubbing his knee, he asked, "What is it you're asking?"

Matt sauntered over to a chair opposite the sofa and then draped his leg over its arm. "I haven't seen you this involved since Carrie," he said.

Joshua stiffened.

Matt had been indirectly involved in the Carrie and Andy Alexander case. He knew how bad it had gone, though he had not been as involved in the case as Angelina had been. "I guess you feel you have to take up the slack since Angelina isn't here?" Joshua asked calmly.

Matt continued to bounce his leg on the arm of the chair. "I know you and Angie are tight, but yeah, she isn't here to keep you on track."

"You think I'm off track?" Joshua asked. He would have sent anyone who was not a member of the team from his office for that insinuation. But the five of them... They all had a special relationship—more like family than co-workers. Each had bonded to the other through many difficult times. You didn't just send a friend like Matt away when he wanted to talk.

Even if you really wanted to at the moment.

"I'm saying, Josh, that I haven't seen you take an interest in anyone like you have Lilly. What is it that has you so wrapped up in her? I mean, we all left work yesterday and come back today and it shows in everything you do. Today during our staff meeting you must have looked at your watch a dozen times. You kept glancing out the window. And as soon as Rita let you know Lilly was here—which in itself is unusual—your entire demeanor changed. And don't tell me that you just wanted to talk to her about her deceit. It was something more."

Joshua relaxed against the plush leather sofa. Running a hand through his hair he admitted defeat. As he'd well known, keeping anything from these guys was almost impossible.

Joshua shifted in his seat. "She reminds me of Carrie."

Matt let out a low whistle.

"Yeah," Joshua said.

"You're not..." Matt hesitated. "You're not thinking she's a replacement...."

"No!" Joshua lowered his voice. "Lilly is a stronger person. I mean, just because I've only found out a hint... It doesn't mean I'm obsessing. I've just noticed how efficient she is, how on top of things as well."

"Something Carrie wasn't ever good at."

Before today Joshua would have snapped at Matt for saying that. But today, for some reason, he was finally able to admit that. "I cared a lot for her. All of you know that. But yeah, she wasn't organized. She did love her child, though...."

"And you still blame yourself for their deaths."

"She didn't trust me enough to stay put,"

Joshua said, low, the old pain and anger rising. "If she'd simply stayed put—"

"You wouldn't have nearly lost your life trying to protect them," Matt interjected.

"They wouldn't have lost *their* lives," Joshua argued even though he rubbed his knee at Matt's words.

Those memories came back, the horror of finding his charges had left the room where he'd told them to stay. Instead they had tried to make a run for it. Out in the open, no way to protect them, he'd ended up watching the mother hit the ground, blood covering her chest.

The only thing he could do as he returned the gunfire was grab the boy, until he'd been shot.

He'd taken three slugs trying to protect Andy as the other agents had come running.

The one to his knee had gone clear through and had killed the boy as well.

For a while, it had been touch and go for him.

At the time he'd wished he had died. All he could remember was the shock on Carrie's face as she hit the ground. Stuck in the middle of the yard as the hit man had fired shot after shot, Joshua had thrust Andy behind him.

He'd thought Andy was okay until he'd fallen, and seen the boy covered in blood as well.

Nightmares had haunted his dreams for the first year. "Look, man," Matt started now. "I know you cared deeply for Carrie and even protected Andy as if he were your own son."

What Matt didn't know was the night before the shooting, Andy had asked Joshua if he could call him Daddy. The pain of that memory would never leave him, though it was only an ache now instead of the intense pain that nearly suffocated him. Thanks to God. Had he not discovered God and what Jesus had done for him, he wasn't sure he would have survived the loss of Carrie and Andy.

"Yeah. Well, that's why I left the business. I crossed the line and got personally involved."

Matt shrugged. What was left unsaid was that because of his knee he would have been forever relegated to a desk job. "It's okay to let go of the past." Matt continued, "Today I saw a look in your eyes that I haven't seen in a long time."

"You're saying I'm involved?"

"Now none of us would fault you. Lilly is quite a looker. We've all been waiting to see you get involved again with someone. The problem I have with it is this. She's hiding something. You don't know what it is. You admitted as much. She's in some sort of danger. It's good to get involved, but you might want to wait until you know more about her situation. Or, at least let the rest of us watch your back."

Joshua said confidently, "I'm not interested in Lilly as anything more than someone who needs protection."

Matt snorted. Both eyebrows going up, he said, "You're not serious with that statement, are you?"

Frowning, Joshua said, "I am."

Matt shook his head. "You have got it bad, my man. You don't even see it, do you?"

Matt dropped his leg to the floor, turning in the chair. Leaning forward in it, he said, "I've got news for you. Your eyes have been opened to the beauty in your front office and your mind is on more than protection. Maybe it's been so long you've forgotten what it is, but I see interest in your eyes when you look at Lilly. And you're going to have to deal with it. Especially since she reminds you of Carrie in some way.''

Angry, Joshua started to ream out Matt for his blunt observations, but then he realized his friend was right. He was interested. A lot. Frustrated that his friend saw how interested he was before he had admitted it to himself, he shifted and crossed his legs. He probably should give Matt some idea of what he'd found out. ''She reminds me of Carrie only in that she is running from something. Carrie was running from the memory of her drug-dealing ex-husband who had been murdered by the mob. I don't think Lilly is involved in anything like that. It seems more—personal—if I had to guess.''

''Which you do because she isn't telling you,'' Matt pointed out.

''She will. She worked for a lawyer in Philadelphia. The building burned down right around the time she quit. She's been running since then. She just found out today that I know this.'' Joshua grinned. ''She wasn't too happy. She's got spunk but she's scared. I wish Angelina was here to get a woman's point of view on what is really going on.'' Running his hand through his hair again, he admitted, ''I walked in on her last night. She was here working. I'd noticed her before, I suppose, but had always been so busy with work....''

''So what was different?''

Joshua chuckled. ''See how she's dressed today?''

Matt affirmed that he had noticed with a grin.

''Exactly. She was here last night doing some work, and I scared her. It was those eyes of hers. She didn't have those glasses on and when you get a look at those eyes—they're so expressive. It was like looking in an open book as we talked. She's attracted to me, though she would never make an advance. I find that odd since over half the women in the company have already made their interests in me very clear.''

''You and me both,'' Matt said, smiling slightly.

"Anyway, I was really surprised by that as well as the fact she has a few morals it seems."

"What'd you do to find that out?" Matt asked, his curiosity piqued.

"Wording," he said, referring to the implied intimacy he'd suggested in her using his given name after hours. "It's not important. What is, however, is that I found a woman who might like me for me. A woman who I am also attracted to."

"The only problem with all of this is that she's hiding a past."

Matt nodded. Then he cocked his head toward the door toward where Lilly sat. "Be careful."

He caught Matt's meaning easily. He wasn't simply telling him to be careful while he tried to discover Lilly's secret. Matt was telling him to be careful with his heart, too.

As angry as he had been earlier at Matt's words, he now deflated and nodded, admitting no matter how interested he found himself in Lilly, his friend was right. "Thanks."

"And when you decide you need help with her—"

"Let me see if she'll tell me first," Joshua said.

Matt nodded. Standing, he headed toward the door. "Later."

"Later."

As the door closed, Joshua Staring realized that after five years something inside him was alive again, something that had been awakened by Lilly Hammond.

And that something was going to be more of a nuisance than he wanted.

"Dear God," he breathed, "why now? It looks like history is repeating itself. I can't be involved and help her work out her problem. It wouldn't be wise. Of course, maybe her problem isn't as bad as I think it is. If that's the case, then getting involved wouldn't be a problem, would it?"

Shaking his head he sighed. "Then again, why did You send her to me and open my eyes if You didn't want me to be involved?"

Standing he walked to the window and stared out at Baton Rouge. It was going to be a long time before he found the answers to the questions he had about Lilly Hammond.

A long time indeed.

Chapter Five

As Matt walked past, Rita walked into Lilly's office. It didn't escape Lilly's notice that Rita gave Matt the once-over as he passed.

If Matt gave her the least little indication, Lilly was sure that Rita would have him at her apartment and in an intimate situation in the blink of an eye.

It grieved Lilly to think Rita might do that. For Rita sex was the answer to her emptiness. She called it dating. Spending time with someone.

Lilly called it what it was…sex outside of marriage. She could call it that and call it sin simply because she had, at one time, been involved like that—until she had become a Christian.

She'd thought sex filled a void and was the thing to be done. She'd enjoyed it, to be sure, but it hadn't filled that empty, hollow space inside of her. She'd tried to talk to Rita about it, but Rita didn't want anything to do with change.

She liked her life the way it was.

She didn't criticize Lilly for her churchgoing ways or because Lilly oftentimes had a Bible on her desk; she just said she wasn't interested.

Seeing her Bible now, Rita asked, "How was church last night?"

"Great."

"You're one of the few people I know who goes to church on Wednesday night."

"I like it." And she did. The singing and teaching was a refreshing time away from the everyday drudgery of office gossip and angry motorists, busy shoppers and irate checkout lines.

Rita chuckled. "So you say."

Lilly knew that Rita would never understand.

Rita ambled across the plush carpet to one of the ornately carved wooden chairs that lined the walls near the desk. Seeing no one else around, she dropped into one. Her stacked red hair didn't even bob as she adjusted herself, crossing her legs, straightening her short, straight tan skirt and jacket. Green eyes scanned Lilly as if looking for something she'd missed before. Lilly had no idea what was going on. "So, what's up with the boss?"

Another thing Lilly didn't like about Rita—Rita loved to gossip. Instead of responding, which she most likely wouldn't have anyway, she avoided Rita's question by asking, "What do you mean?" Lilly resumed sorting the information she'd compiled on generators.

"He was very distracted when he came in this morning. And he was late." Rita blinked her eyes, opening them a bit wider, attempting an innocent, concerned expression. "I beat him into work. He's a workaholic. He's usually here before anyone. I hope he isn't sick…or something."

"I don't know, Rita. Maybe he is," Lilly commented, grateful it was that easy to answer. She should have known better.

"Then he contacts me and wants to know as soon as you arrive. And when you do arrive, you come in dressed...well, beau," she said pronouncing it *boo*, a common Cajun term, Lilly had learned. "You normally look like you're stating to the world *hands off*. But today you come in and you're dressed much differently. Pink and fuzzy instead of dark and professional...and the boss is asking about you...."

Lilly suddenly realized where Rita was going. "You're dead wrong, Rita. There is nothing going on between Mr. Staring and me. I was working late, after church. I've been having trouble sleeping. Anyway, he came in and found me here." That wasn't really a lie, Lilly thought. He did know she was terrified of phone calls in the middle of the night—thanks to Angelina's untimely call. "Anyway, I'm sure he was simply concerned."

Rita's gaze sharpened. Before she could comment, however, Joshua came out of his office. "Lilly, make an appointment for the two of us for lunch. Pick wherever you want to go. I have some corporate information we need to review," he said.

She opened her mouth but Joshua was gone, back into his office.

Weakly she glanced back over at Rita who was staring at her with a gaze full of innuendo. "You were just saying..." she said knowingly.

"Rita," Lilly warned, low.

Rita chuckled, ignoring Lilly's distress. "I have to get back to work. Let me know how it goes."

Lilly watched Rita hurry out of the office. She was certain Rita was on her way to share her scoop with all the other secretaries on the fourth floor. It would only be a matter of time before the entire company heard the gossip.

Joshua was a very private individual.

So was she.

Neither one of them would like their names bandied about like that.

But it was better, she supposed, than the alternative. Rita could have found out that Joshua had grilled her about her past. Or she could have found out that Lilly was running *from* her past.

Yeah, she thought miserably, Rita could have found out so many things.

Wearily Lilly leaned forward, resting her elbows on her desk and her forehead against her folded hands. Things had been going so well until last night.

She hadn't expected anyone, that was for sure. Joshua had startled her, getting underneath her armor, sneaking in and grabbing a peak at the real her.

Each morning Lilly took extra care dressing. She got up and showered, dried her long hair and then painfully pulled it up, pinning it back on her head. She knew that her hair pulled back like that would suggest to others that she was in control and didn't need help. She'd carefully chosen her wardrobe to reflect professionalism. She wanted no one to mistake her for someone full of fears and needs on the inside. She wanted to look confident.

She'd even chosen glasses to wear. Her prescription wasn't that bad. Wearing the glasses, the bigger ones that took up a lot of her face, hid her eyes—eyes that Taylor had once told her gave away her inner thoughts.

The look in Joshua's eyes last night, the concern… She didn't want to get him killed like her last boss. Joshua had no idea what he was getting into, how bad Taylor was or just how much power he wielded. But even if he had known, her last boss had been a lawyer, a gentle, kind man who had wanted to help. She wasn't sure this man would have the contacts necessary to stop Taylor.

She'd told him about Taylor, but before anything could be done, he'd been killed. Taylor had seen to that.

She thought hiding out here at a security firm was the perfect answer. And in many ways, it was. The fear of something happening again to her boss had been kept at bay until last night.

Joshua was former FBI. Most of those men were arrogant and nasty—at least to Taylor and his followers. Joshua didn't seem that way, however. She wanted to talk to him. She was tired of running, tired of living out of a suitcase. Could Joshua help? But what if Taylor found out? She'd heard the rumors that Joshua had lost someone on a case and that's why he limped.

She didn't want to put him in that danger again. He most likely didn't want to be in that position again either. But which would be more dangerous? Telling him or keeping quiet?

So, this morning she'd packed her bags, loaded her car and actually started to leave town. As she'd started to run she'd realized Joshua would find her. He'd promised that he would and the look in his eyes—a look of absolute authority and certainty—had convinced her of it.

So, right there on I-10 she'd turned around, trying to make it back to the office without being late. She should have gone home and changed first—it would have been less obvious what she'd been about to do. She'd only thought about getting back before he sent out word to find her or before she gave in to her fears and keep going.

She wasn't sure what he would have done, but she knew Joshua was someone who would act. He wouldn't back down from something once he'd tossed down the gauntlet.

What she hadn't been ready for was the questions this morning when she'd gotten into work. She should have realized, of course, he would have checked up on her. He knew about the lawyer and that she was connected in some way to his death. He didn't know about her other name and the time she'd spent in the retreat, as Taylor had called it.

Not yet, at least.

Despite checking up on her, however, she did still see his concern—and interest.

What was so awful, however, was that she returned his interest. She hadn't felt anything since those first few months with Taylor—before she'd realized his deceit and before she had changed her whole view of the man she'd thought she loved.

Joshua was a larger than life type of hero from Pride, Louisiana. She'd done her own discreet checking up on him. Born and raised in the small town just north of Baton Rouge, both of his parents were dead. He'd inherited the house, which he called the bunker, from them. Not happy with small-town life he'd gone off to join the navy, ending up in the FBI. But the injury to his knee had effectively ended his career.

He was back in town, running a business with his friends who had also been in various government jobs. He was a Christian, went to church and was considered a good but elusive catch.

At least for everyone except Lilly, it seemed.

Rita was right.

There was something going on between them—just since last night.

And she wasn't sure what it was.

But rumors were going to be running rampant—and soon.

Glancing down at what she was wearing she decided the best way to end those rumors, or at least help quell them, was to change.

And since she had her clothes packed in her car downstairs, it wouldn't take any time at all to do that.

Ringing Joshua, she waited for him to answer.

"Yes, Lilly?"

A slight flush touched her cheeks. He'd called her by her last name so long, Lilly just sounded so intimate in an office setting. "I have to go down to my car for something. I'll be back in about fifteen minutes. I'll forward the telephones to Kelly's desk. If you need anything, buzz her, please."

"Will do."

"Lunch reservations will be at Cactus Café if that's okay."

"Sounds great."

She hung up the phone. He was at work in there. Short succinct answers. Just the way he'd been for the last months she'd worked for him.

At least that was back to normal.

Her telephone buzzed.

"Yes?" she said, picking up Joshua's private line to her.

"I'm looking forward to lunch, so don't run off."

The phone clicked.

She hung up her own phone.

Well, she thought, almost back to normal.

After she forwarded the phones and informed Kelly she would be away from her desk for a few minutes, Lilly got up and walked to the elevator. Eyes watched her as she went. Inwardly sighing, she thought that this was as normal as things were going to get.

Chapter Six

So, you have a new protector, do you? I would have thought you'd learned with the last one. Obviously, you haven't.

A security firm.

Don't you realize I'm invincible, sunshine? I have powers on my side that will see me through this, powers you can't even imagine—or can you? I have a following that will bow and scrape and do whatever I command, though you, I had kept for my own pleasure. You'll pay for that defection, however, by my own hands.

I see you digging in your suitcase, my

beauty. So, you've thought about leaving, but someone there must have convinced you to stay.

Who is it that you have on your side now? Who knows your dirty little secret?

I'd wager no one, knowing you. You're ashamed of your past, aren't you, sweet one? That only gives me an advantage. As long as you aren't telling, that gives me power.

You look up suddenly as if you sense me, can hear my cruel laughter once again. Do you? Can you hear me laughing?

You will soon, Lilly.

I'm here.

I've come for you.

Chapter Seven

He would have laughed except that he knew she'd ask why he was laughing.

Joshua hadn't expected to find the "old Lilly" sitting at her desk when he walked out of his office for lunch.

But that's exactly what he found.

Dark charcoal suit, glasses in place, hair pulled back with two sticks holding it up, Lilly sat there, in her full armor, typing away.

"Ready to go?" he asked, acting as nonchalantly as possible.

She glanced at him as if expecting more. He saw it out of the corner of his eye. So he didn't give it to her. Best way to get back under that defense was to keep her off balance.

"Yes, sir."

She picked up her phone and forwarded it to reception and then grabbed her purse from the bottom drawer of her desk.

He opened her office door, nodding to Nancy, who worked the main desk in this area.

He noted Kelly and Rita at the overflow office staring intently as they walked by.

Looked like the rumor mill was at it again.

He knew Rita was a gossip and looking for a husband. He wasn't surprised she'd notice a change in routine for him. And if taking Lilly out wasn't a change in routine, he didn't know what was.

It didn't matter that he carried his black leather briefcase with him. Somehow those in the office who made his personal life their business would have forgotten that by the time they spread the news that something new was going on.

Poor Lilly.

She didn't want attention but he'd just put her in the middle of it by walking out with her.

As he passed Todd's office he noted Todd standing there, mug in hand, watching him walk down the hall. Todd lifted the cup in silent salute before taking a sip.

He was really going to have to have a talk with Todd about listening to rumors.

"I hope you don't mind the stares," he said as they approached the elevator.

Lilly punched the button, not looking down the hall toward the people they'd passed, but gazing straight ahead. "I'm sorry, Mr.... Joshua. It's my fault. Rita came over earlier. My dramatic change in attire attracted her attention."

"Rita," he murmured, seeing he'd guessed right.

"I changed, but it was too late. I'm sure they're saying all kinds of things by now. I know you like your privacy—"

"Privacy, yes. Personal life? I'm afraid, Lilly, dear, that this isn't anything new for me. It was like this before you came. Don't you know, according to the secretarial pool, I'm the dark brooding type in need of a woman to straighten me out?"

He saw her eyes widen and grinned.

The elevator arrived and they stepped inside.

It was rather funny when they turned. All the way back down the hall, he could see heads craned, watching them. Purposely he reached around Lilly to push the down button, forcing her into what might look like a close cuddling embrace.

"Excuse me," he murmured as the doors closed.

"You did that on purpose," Lilly accused, glaring up at him in astonishment and reproach.

He chuckled, thoroughly enjoying Lilly's outrage. "Gotta give the gossips something to talk about while we're at lunch. Besides, do you really care what they think?"

Lilly opened her mouth to complain, then glanced around. "How did you know what the women say in the break room?"

Joshua burst out laughing. "You think I've got it bugged?"

Lilly scowled. "Well, you were pretty accurate about what they say."

He shook his head, still chuckling. "If only I did," he murmured, grinning.

The elevator doors opened and they walked out. He nodded to the security guard, to clients waiting for appointments with his colleagues and then at the cameras he was sure Todd and that group were watching before turning down a side hall. His team. A good lot, but way too nosy.

Leading Lilly out the side door, he walked across the muggy parking lot. He unlocked the passenger door of the silver Mercedes sedan and opened it, waiting for Lilly to slide in.

Closing it once she was settled, he walked around to the back door on the driver's side. Setting his briefcase down he slipped his jacket off, pulled the back door open and slipped the conservative jacket onto a hanger. Grabbing his briefcase he placed it on the back seat along with his walking stick and then shut the door.

In seconds he was in the driver's seat and had the car running.

Adjusting the air conditioner, he reached up and loosened his tie. "It's sure humid out to-day."

Lilly nodded. "Clouds are building. Hope-fully it'll cool off some once the sun is blocked."

"We'll have rain by three o'clock," he added.

Resting his white-clad right arm along the back of Lilly's seat, he glanced over his shoulder and backed out. When he was clear of the other cars he turned around. Both hands on the wheel, he drove the car out of the parking area. Reaching up, he hit a small button on a thin square security pad he kept on his visor, which opened the gate.

A quick stop for traffic and then they were on their way toward Baker, Louisiana, a small suburb that had the best Mexican food this side of the Mississippi.

"What was it you wanted to discuss?"

Joshua glanced briefly at Lilly. She didn't like the quiet. She'd done the same thing last night. When things got too quiet and she felt nervous or out of control, she liked to seize the moment and try to mold it into something she could control.

That was fine with him because Joshua knew that Lilly's control was simply a facade. Real control came from within, not the situation around a person. "The quarterly budget.

We've run into some unexpected problems and it looks like we're going to have to do some shuffling. The different departments gave you some reports last week. I want your input on the administrative end.''

''My input?''

He'd surprised her. Smiling he nodded. ''You're very efficient, Lilly. I'd like to find out just where you feel there's waste or where we have real needs. Some of the reports I've gotten from the departments seem a bit inflated. I'd like your advice. But it can wait until after lunch.''

Lilly folded her hands in her lap. The seat belt held her securely as she clasped her hands and thought about what he'd said.

''And I just wanted time to get to know you better,'' he added softly just as she'd started to relax.

Those hands clasped each other again and she stiffened. A slight flush touched her cheeks giving him a warm feeling inside. She liked his attention, though it made her nervous.

He wondered what she'd think if he admitted it made him nervous, too. He'd really like to know more about her, but he didn't want to push her too fast.

Being pushy might hurt his chances with her. In today's society, all she'd really have to do was say back off and he'd have to, or else he could get slapped with a harassment suit.

He probably would not have acted on his attraction if he hadn't realized she returned some sort of feelings.

"I, well...Joshua," she finally said, and there was despair in her voice.

"You're a good woman, Lilly Hammond. Obviously you're caught up in a bad situation. But, you're a good woman."

"You don't know everything about me," she whispered when he didn't go on.

Joshua turned off the highway and onto Highway 19, the main street of Baker. "If I know you twenty years I'll never know everything about you," he said quietly. "That's life."

"That's not what I meant," she countered.

He paused at a stoplight. "I know it, Lilly. But you also know I'm here to listen, whenever you want to talk."

He didn't think she was going to answer.

The light turned green.

He drove another half mile before she said, so softly, that had they been anywhere but the interior of his quiet car, he would have missed it, "I'm scared."

His heart clenched.

To see this confident woman who took control of so many situations admit, for the first time to him, that she was scared, made him want to slay dragons. It made him angry that someone would produce feelings like that in someone so tiny and delicate.

She should have been protected and nurtured. Instead, she was running and afraid, unable to have a normal life.

"I know you are." He said it simply and with finality.

"I want to tell you," she added, a bit stronger.

That a girl, he thought, smiling inwardly at her courage.

"I just can't."

Her words didn't discourage him. Instead, they gave him hope. "You will, in time, when you feel it's safe."

Out of the corner of his eye he saw the relief flood her features. She realized he understood. When she felt safe she'd tell him. There was only one way for that to happen. He had to get to know her better. That was part of the reason he had planned this lunch. He wanted to earn her trust. She would tell him when she was ready.

Trying to change the mood in the car she smiled and said, "If I tell you mine you have to tell me yours."

He chuckled and then nodded. "That's only fair."

Of course, he didn't have to tell her everything. He was certain she knew some about what had happened. But she didn't need to know his fear of meeting a woman who wouldn't listen, who would put her life and his in danger as Carrie had.

He could live with telling her just about anything else. And he would, if it would help him get to know her better.

The reason was simple. He found himself entranced by this woman. He'd asked God in prayer why He had sent this woman his way.

He was finding that maybe God knew what He was doing.

Maybe it was time for him to have his foundation shaken, to wake up. Maybe it was time for him to start living again and Lilly Hammond was definitely someone that could reach inside him and ignite the long-dormant flame of life.

Chapter Eight

Rita lay in wait for her when Lilly returned to her office.

Of course, to the outsider it looked as if Rita were simply there to give Lilly a report—she was going to have to have a talk with Nancy about letting the other secretaries in here when she wasn't here—but Lilly knew Rita was really there to question her.

Glad Joshua had stopped by Davie's office, which was really not an office at all, Lilly put on a smile and strode forward toward her desk. Davie's real office was next door, but Joshua had gone to the computer level of their build-

ing, knowing that was where he would find
Davie.

"What's up?" she asked Rita as she replaced her purse in her desk drawer. Seating
herself, she accepted the files Rita handed her.

"These are from Mr. Martin," Rita said referring to Matt. Lilly knew the bosses better by
their first names, hearing Joshua refer to them
that way all the time. However, she was the
only one. Everyone else knew the partners
strictly by their last name—except when
Joshua went barreling down the hall yelling
"Angelina!"

Glancing at the files in her hand, she noted
they were updated security reports.

"I'll see to them when Mr. Staring returns."

Rita didn't take the hint. Dropping down in
a seat, she asked, "So, how was lunch?"

A loaded question. Lilly had a wonderful
time talking with Joshua. She didn't think she
should tell Rita that, however. Carefully, she
replied, "We got a lot of work done."

"Oh, yeah. Sure, honey," Rita said and
chuckled. "I can tell by the glow in your
eyes."

Lilly wondered if it was true and Rita could really see the excitement reflected there. Carefully she adjusted her glasses.

"I have to tell you," Rita continued, "lunch here was awful. Kelly was supposed to bring the meal today—she had leftover soup—but she forgot it. So we ate out of the machines. Mexican sounds wonderful. I think I'll go for some tonight and since I'm sharing lunch with Kelly tomorrow, I just might bring the leftovers into the office. Did you know Kelly is allergic to chili powder?"

Lilly couldn't help but laugh. "You will not, Rita Muñoz!" Covering her mouth she shook her head. "You're awful."

Rita only laughed. "But you love me."

Lilly wouldn't go that far, but unfortunately, she did like the woman. When she finally stopped laughing she said, "I give up. You're right. I had a great lunch. Mr. Staring is really nice company."

Rita nodded. "I knew he would be. He has *gentleman* written all over him."

Lilly's heart contracted at the wistful sound in Rita's voice.

"If only *I* could find a man like that."

"You're looking in the wrong places, Rita," Lilly replied softly.

Rita waved a hand. "There are good guys that hang out at the clubs, too. Besides, the guy you went to lunch with is at work, not a bar."

Lilly sighed. She wanted to ask if Rita had ever looked twice at Davie, who had definitely noticed her, but then, that would be going too far. If those two couldn't see it, she wasn't going to push it. "You've got me there," Lilly only said.

Joshua walked in and Rita fell quiet.

His eyes floated across Rita to Lilly and the look of amusement in his eyes told her that he knew he had been the topic of discussion. Everyone knew Rita enjoyed chatting. About everything. Lilly thought it was because Rita was really lonely.

If she'd only accept Jesus....

"Type those notes up and I want a report on my desk by 4:00 p.m. today."

Lilly nodded.

The door closed behind him.

Rita sighed. "What a hunk."

Lilly shook her head. "I have to get to work."

Grinning, Rita stood. "I'm going to catch you after work and then you're really going to have to tell me what went on at lunch."

"Go!" Lilly said sweetly, Rita's grin infectious.

When she was gone, Lilly thought back to what went on during lunch.

Cactus Café had been crowded, but they'd reserved a table for Joshua. She and Joshua had sat back in the corner of the nonsmoking section. A TV above their heads had blared the local news. People around them had eaten and chatted while harried waitresses ran back and forth, seeing that everyone had what they needed.

But she and Joshua had seemed isolated. He'd pulled out her chair for her, put his back to the wall so she had to face him and the world had faded.

Nothing personal had actually been discussed, just business. But in some way something had changed. The walls between them didn't seem so thick now. Joshua seemed more like a *Joshua* than a *Mr. Staring*. She liked the way his eyes crinkled when he smiled and those deep dimples appeared. When he listened he gave her his full attention, not just tolerating her but actually listening.

He'd been intrigued by some of her ideas. He'd asked questions and made mental notes, asking other questions and poking holes in her suggestions until he'd ironed out some strategies.

Then he'd taken a small notebook out of his briefcase and made two pages of quick notes and handed them to her, expecting her to remember everything else.

When dinner was over he'd paid and they'd returned to his car. The quiet easy silence on the way back had been something she wasn't used to. She didn't normally like the quiet, but after the meal, the small talk and the undercurrents that flowed between them, she accepted it.

Now back at the office all she wanted to do was dwell on Joshua, but instead, she had work to do. Although she wasn't quite sure how she was going to get it all done.

"Ahem."

Glancing up she realized Todd had somehow walked right into her office and to the front of her desk without her realizing it.

She felt heat rising in her cheeks. "Can I help you?" she asked, embarrassed that she had to ask such a thing.

"Is Josh busy?" he asked in those cultured British tones of his.

She buzzed Joshua. "Mr. Staring, Todd Ashcroft is here to see you."

"Send him in."

She wasn't sure, but the sound of Joshua's voice was almost certainly long suffering at best.

Todd must have thought so, too, because he tipped his coffee cup at her in acknowledgment. Chuckling, he strode past into the office.

As the door opened, she heard, "I was planning to talk to you...."

"Oh?" Todd said, closing the door behind him.

Joshua saw Todd carried the same, infernal black cup with which he'd saluted him earlier.

Leaning back in his chair, Joshua steepled his fingers and smiled. To anyone else his expression would look predatory, but his pensive attitude didn't deter Todd. Joshua was glad his secretary wasn't in his office right now to see him. He'd enjoyed her company at lunch too much to have her running scared again.

Todd lifted his eyebrows as if to say, *Is that look for me?*

Joshua didn't deign to answer. Instead, he asked, "What are the rumors that had you glued to your door when I went out to lunch?"

Todd grinned. "The lovely lady outside."

"I thought I made it clear this morning—"

"Oh, my yes," Todd said and chuckled. "You made it quite clear—to all of us, if not to yourself."

"Spare me," Joshua said mildly. "I've already heard it from Matt."

"I shouldn't be surprised," Todd replied. "Someone has to keep you in line since our mother is gone."

"Angelina would have your hide in small strips if she heard you call her that and you know it."

Todd's smile faded. "Before you tear into me about my teasing salute, we need to talk."

Joshua's need to do exactly what Todd had said faded. His need for payback was replaced with a sense of foreboding. "What's up?"

"Angelina hasn't checked in."

Joshua stilled.

He knew exactly what Todd was intimating. Angelina was a professional. She might have gone somewhere without telling them the details, but she would have checked in, if it was possible.

"How long has it been?" He calculated when he'd spoken with her.

"According to Davie she should have arrived in Australia four hours ago."

She must have been on the plane this morning when Davie dropped the bombshell about Australia, he realized. "Four hours isn't too long. Her ride could have been delayed. She might have to travel a bit to wherever she's going."

Todd frowned. "She would have called."

Joshua couldn't help but share Todd's unease. They'd gone through a lot together. A former Special Agent in charge of White House security, Angie was one tough cookie. She'd still be there today if things hadn't gone wrong two years ago....

"Do you have any idea why she went to Australia?"

Joshua shook his head. "I imagine if Davie did, he would have mentioned it by now," he surmised. "Perhaps you might get in touch with some of your old contacts from the agency and see if anything noteworthy has been going on at the Hill...or anywhere else that might tie in to Angie's trip."

"Exactly what I wanted to do," Todd affirmed.

"Great." Joshua tried to quell his worry. "Angelina is a strong person, able to take care of herself. If she needs us, she'll call."

He hoped if he kept saying that, he'd believe it.

"Right," Todd agreed, sounding about as sure as Joshua felt. "So, what did you want to talk to me about?"

Forcing his mind back to the person at hand, namely Lilly Hammond, he remembered their lunch today and her problem. "I think the lady wants to talk. However, I need..." He hesitated, then plunged ahead, "Advice on just how to break the ice."

"Oh-ho," Todd said and chuckled.

Joshua squirmed. "I knew I shouldn't have asked."

"No, you came to the right person." Todd actually preened, grinning as he did.

Joshua lobbed a pen at him. "Forget it."

Todd lifted a hand and worked to control his laughter. "No. No, wait. It's just...Mr. Eligible here and you need advice. It's too funny. I mean...all you'd have to do is step out that door and give any woman 'the look' and you'd have them waiting in line...."

"Todd..." Joshua warned. He felt the tips of his ears reddening.

"Okay. Really. I'm sorry. I mean it. This time," he added, obviously interpreting Joshua's look of disbelief correctly.

"Let me ask you something." Todd forced his laughter aside and studied his friend.

Joshua didn't like questions, but Todd seemed to be calming down. "Go ahead."

"You had no trouble with Carrie. Why suddenly are you worried about this woman?"

Joshua sighed. Rubbing his sore knee, he commented, "This is different."

Todd didn't say anything, but took a sip from his ceramic mug and waited for Joshua to enlighten him. "First off, she's my secretary. One wrong step and I could be slapped with a harassment suit."

"She doesn't look the type to do that," Todd said briefly.

"I don't think so. But she is skittish. Secondly, it's been...well...years since I've dated."

"That's why we're all watching with baited breath," Todd said dryly. "Next?"

Joshua scowled. Here was the real problem—the reason he felt so inadequate. "She didn't respond in any way to me at lunch."

Todd lifted an eyebrow in surprise. "The devil, you say."

Acutely uncomfortable, Joshua suddenly wondered why he was asking Todd for help. He should have just left well enough alone. But he couldn't.

"She's attracted to you, Josh. I mean, when I came up to your office just now, she was in a daydream, a thousand miles from here. I actually had to clear my throat to get her attention. I found it amusing, actually."

"Don't give Lilly a hard time," Joshua warned.

Responding seriously to Joshua's warning, Todd replied, "Of course not."

Joshua sighed wearily and ran a hand through his hair. "Sorry. I know you wouldn't. I am just...well...I had wanted to get to know her but suddenly, at lunch, I found I had no idea what to ask her."

"What did you talk about?" Todd asked curiously.

"The quarterly budget reports. She had some fascinating ideas and I wanted to hear her out. I—"

"Uh, Josh..." Todd interrupted.

Joshua nodded. "Exactly." Sighing he said, "We talked for nearly two hours and it was all business."

"You said she didn't respond to you," Todd prompted.

"I listened. We talked. I did ask her if she liked sushi, but I didn't want to get too personal. She is my secretary and if I push too hard—"

Todd sighed. "You are always too worried about what other people think. At least, since Carrie. Listen…"

He paused, holding up a hand when Joshua started to argue the point. "No. Listen. Carrie is part of the reason you ended up quitting your job and moving back here to Baton Rouge. You felt that it never looked right that you had gotten involved with someone you were assigned to protect—someone who died on your watch. Since then you've held yourself aloof from everyone who tries to approach you. It sounds like that's all the problem is here."

"If only it were that easy," Joshua muttered.

Todd lifted an eyebrow. He took a sip of his tea and then set his mug down on Joshua's desk. Leaning forward, resting his hands on his knees, he said, "Want me to show you that's all it is?"

"Okay," Joshua said, expecting Todd to make a fool of himself in some way. He, of course, should have known his ever unflappable American-born British-sounding friend would never do such a thing. Instead, he smiled and said, "Invite her to the bunker for supper."

Joshua blinked. "Do what?"

Todd smiled at him. Leaning back in his chair he crossed his legs. "You won't because you're too worried about what people will think. Up until now you can explain everything away and laugh at all of the talk. After all, you only discussed business. But if you invite her over to your house, fix her a meal and spend time with her, then... The gossips will have every right to tie you two together. And you just can't handle that."

Joshua scowled, his anger building. "That's not right, Todd, and you know it."

Todd shrugged. "You won't do it."

Joshua nodded. "That's right. And not because it wouldn't look right...."

"Then why?" he asked bluntly.

Joshua couldn't think of a reply.

He was saved when his phone buzzed. "Joshua, Angelina is on line one."

Saved, Todd mouthed.

Joshua didn't admit it or deny it. Instead, he turned his attention to the phone and Angelina, unwilling to closely examine why he couldn't invite Lilly to his house.

Chapter Nine

Entering her house, Lilly dumped her briefcase in the chair by her front door. Kicking off her shoes, she set the last of her suitcases down next to the TV. Reaching up on the front door, she snagged a note from her landlord. It explained why he hadn't been able to fix the oven again.

It had been a long day—a very long day. Actually, it seemed like two days, considering that's how long it had taken her to bring *both* of her suitcases in from the car. Bringing in the last suitcase signified her acceptance that she was staying here. It was a finality of sorts.

She closed the door and dropped the note on a small table next to the door. She loved it here, but the landlord was slow on getting things done. He was a good man, however, just over-worked.

Today, though, she didn't care to worry about such things.

Crossing the tightly woven tan carpet, she reached up and pulled the rod from her hair, releasing the long strands. Running both hands through the brown curls, she rubbed the sore spots made by her hairpins.

She flopped down on the multicolored, earth-toned sofa that she'd found for a cheap price at an outlet store and grabbed the TV remote, which she'd discarded haphazardly on the cushions that morning before leaving for work.

Flipping on the TV, she turned to the local news while she unbuttoned her jacket.

A woman on the screen reported the death and destruction going on around them. Nothing new in that, Lilly thought sadly as she slipped the jacket from her shoulders.

Laying the remote on the table next to the

couch, she tossed the jacket on the chair across from the sofa.

Stretching, her back actually popped. "Stored-up stress," she murmured.

She glanced back at her suitcase and she decided that she would wait to unpack. Feeling restless, she got up, grabbed the suitcases one at a time and carried them down the hall to her bedroom. There she laid them on her bed. She opened them, flipped the lid back and then returned to the living room.

The man on the screen was now reporting on a house fire.

She shuddered.

She hated fires.

Going into her kitchen to find something to eat, she thought again of the last two days at work.

After Rita had left, Lilly had started on her work. She'd noted an unusual amount of traffic back and forth from Joshua's office.

They were all worried about Angelina, it seemed.

She wasn't sure what was going on, but from what she could gather, Angelina was in Aus-

tralia and all of the bosses were worried—
which meant she wasn't there on business.

Today things had been somewhat back to
normal, except for one missing boss—Angelina—and the fact that the entire fourth-floor
crew watched Lilly with some sort of expec-
tation.

Joshua treated Lilly with the utmost respect,
never crossing the line, but there was something in his gaze—something that made her
nervous just the same.

Not nervous in a bad way, just…nervous.

The bosses had their meeting on the quarterly budget and several of the suggestions
were discussed. She'd noticed first Matt and
then Davie looking at her with expressions that
suggested they knew she'd helped Joshua with
the ideas they'd discussed. Davie's look of be-
trayal had been the funniest. He used his young
looks well with most people, fooling them.
She, however, knew that he was much world-
lier than he let on, so that hurt-boy look didn't
work with her.

She heard the commercial on the TV end
and the weather report come on. Pausing in her

foray into the freezer, she returned to the living room, dropping onto the sofa.

There was a ninety percent chance of rain, the forecaster said.

As if on cue, she heard thunder.

And then the forecaster gave a report on Hurricane Isis. Surprised, she saw that the storm, which was a category two, was now pounding the Bahamas. Chewing her lip, she noted the storm's trajectory.

It definitely looked like it was coming into the Gulf, which meant they were going to have rain. Not the small weather pattern that had brought the rain today, but some heavy rain.

She'd studied up on hurricanes since last night, doing extensive research on the Web during her breaks. She felt a bit silly now for worrying about this, realizing that places like Tampa, Mobile, Pensacola and Brownsville were all hit quite often. New Orleans wasn't. And Baton Rouge was so far inland that, from what she could find on the Web, they weren't in danger at all.

She had much to learn about the area.

Taking off her glasses, she rubbed her eyes.

The glasses were actually invisible line bifocals. She used them for reading and computer work but didn't need them for anything else, so she didn't really have to wear them.

The sound of rain outside proved the forecast should have been one hundred percent for rain today instead of only ninety. Of course, any prediction over about twenty percent usually meant rain here, she thought amusedly. Leaning back, she listened to the sudden downpour and smiled.

One thing she had learned about Baton Rouge—it got over sixty inches of rain a year. It was like living in the tropics. Always hot and humid and rainy. She couldn't wait to see what the winters were like.

The phone rang.

Still smiling over the idea of being here for winter she snagged the phone. "Hello?"

Her smile fled when no one answered.

Someone was on the line but not answering. "Who is this?" she asked, then suddenly she was afraid the person on the other end might answer. She slammed the phone down.

All thoughts of the peaceful-sounding rain

fled, replaced by killer tension as muscle by muscle she tightened up.

The rain sounded menacing all of a sudden. It would cover anyone coming up the sidewalk, anyone who might be standing outside her door. The sound of the incessant downpour could cover any noise that might alert her to danger.

Jerking the telephone back up she quickly dialed a number to find out who had called, but the recorded voice told her it was out of the area.

She slammed the phone down again. Shivering, she stared at it...and waited.

And waited.

It rang again.

She'd known it would.

It was happening all over again. Just like in Philadelphia. Just like before the fire...

She reached for the receiver, lifted it up just high enough so the call connected, then dropped it back on its hook.

Shuddering, she wrapped her arms around herself. She didn't want this. She hated this. What had she done to deserve this?

The phone rang again. Jerking it up, she quickly slammed it back down.

Knowing that wouldn't stop whomever it was, she lunged back to the phone and with a near sob, jerked it off the hook.

As the dial tone and then the beeping of an off-the-hook phone played out their tune, Lilly cried out her own song of fear.

Shivering on the sofa, tears running down her face, sobs escaped as she fought the desire to run.

"He's always going to find me, God. I can't escape. What am I going to do? I can't go back. I won't. He knows that. So why does he keep hunting me down? What does he want with me?"

She thought of going to the police. But what could she tell them? She'd tried that in Philadelphia, and look how well that had worked.

Her hands were icy and she felt chilled to the bone.

"I don't know what to do," she whispered in prayer to her heavenly father. "Abba, Father, guide me," she whispered, calling her father by the more intimate term. "Please help me."

Realizing her teeth were chattering, she forced herself to stand.

She wasn't going to sit here on the sofa and cower. She'd end up sick by morning if she did. Instead, she'd force herself to go on, step by step. God would help her, He would see to her safety, though she wasn't sure how or what He would have her do.

She just had to trust Him.

Still fearful though not panicked like she was when the phone rang, she forced herself to concentrate on one thing at a time. First thing she wanted to do was warm up.

Despite it being seventy degrees in the house, she was cold. She knew it was in re-action to the calls. The sick jerk was out there somewhere, doing his best to terrorize her, but she wasn't going to let him. So, to warm her-self up and to relieve the tension, she'd shower. It was a first step in many to come. After show-ering, she'd sit down and see what came to mind as a plan of action against Taylor. Then she'd go from there.

Going into her bedroom she grabbed up some warm fuzzy sweats and headed into the bathroom.

Her wardrobe, she'd found out quickly after arriving in Baton Rouge, was all wrong for the area. But wearing her sweats around in the evening was something she couldn't give up—even if it meant turning the air-conditioning up to make the apartment just a bit cooler.

Stepping into the shower she made the water scalding hot. The hot water was a shock to her body, but it did, almost immediately, chase away the chill that had settled into her bones.

She lifted her face, allowing the warm stream to hit her as she continued to pray about what to do.

When the hot water finally ran out, she stepped from the shower and dried off, slipped on her sweats and headed back into the living room. She felt much warmer now. The chill was gone. And her muscles weren't so tight that they were pulling her bones to the point that she creaked! Now, for the next step in her plan.

Or so she thought. Walking into the living room, she stopped short. A shadow passed by the window on the left side of her door and stopped right outside.

She gasped as her mind and body both frozc in place. All thoughts of planning fled as she realized someone stood out there. Had Taylor finally done it? Had he finally decided to confront her?

Before she could think of what to do, someone pounding on the wooden structure shattered the silence.

She shouldn't have showered. She should havc called someone—even the police. Who cared if they didn't listen to her, she realized now. At least they'd have a report, so if she went missing—

"Lilly? Are you in there?"

Her mouth dropped open. That wasn't the voice of her tormentor, but of her quiet hero. It couldn't be. Barely above a whisper, she squeaked out, "Joshua?"

Shaking her head, the fear suddenly gone, replaced with utter shock, she moved toward the door.

"Lilly?" He pounded on the door again obviously not having heard her weak attempt at a reply.

"Joshua?" she said again, louder, and moved until she could look out the peephole.

Joshua stood there, getting soaked, she realized, from the fierce rain.

Getting soaked.

Oh, heavens!

Quickly unlocking the barrier between them, she pulled it open.

He didn't wait for an invitation but strode into her house and space, coming within inches of her. She backpedaled, but he kept coming. Gripping her by both shoulders, his long black cane hit her in the back as his gaze swept over her. "Are you okay?"

Hard eyes examined her, looking, searching her as if he expected to find her injured. Water soaked through her sweat suit top. It dripped onto the floor from his dark soaked head.

"I—I—I'm fine," she stuttered when he jarred her with his hands.

"You slammed the phone in my ear—twice. And then I couldn't get you at all."

Glancing around, his gaze landed on the phone next to the sofa on the small table and the receiver, which lay off the hook. Muttering something under his breath, he strode across the room, the cane making his gait almost even.

He picked the receiver up in his hand. Turning toward her, he said softly, slowly, "Never, *ever,* take the phone off the hook like this. If you were in trouble, no one could get hold of you."

She swallowed and nodded.

He quietly hung the phone up and then, reaching up with his right hand, slicked back his soaking wet hair.

Oh, dear. "Stay right there," she said apologetically and hurried past him into the hallway.

Opening a cabinet, she pulled out a plush, terry cloth towel. When she closed the cabinet, she jumped, squawking.

Joshua had followed her. "Here," she said, thrusting the towel at him.

At least he looked a bit disconcerted at having a towel shoved in his face—but only for a moment. He took the towel and rubbed his clean-cut features with those two familiar dimples that always appeared when he smiled—but were most obviously absent right now—and then the towel moved to his hair. When he proceeded to strip his shirt off as he walked back into the living room, she gaped.

Swallowing loudly, knowing her eyes looked like owl eyes, she started after him.

Then he walked into her kitchen and out of sight. What in the world did he think he was doing? He was in her kitchen, barechested and doing what? Cooking?

She hurried after him.

He stood at her sink, wringing out his top before slipping it back on and buttoning it up.

Joshua knew she was there. He simply ignored her. As she watched, she became perturbed. This was her apartment. She shouldn't be watching him. He should be watching her.

Confused, she shook her head. Well, something like that. "May I ask what you are doing here?" she demanded.

At the look on his face, she realized why he was so quiet. It was because he was furious.

She turned to go back into the living room, not certain she wanted to hear what had brought him there after all.

She didn't make it into the living room. Joshua's strong hand clamped around her tiny upper arm and pulled her back around. "We need to talk."

She wanted to argue, but the utter look of authority and knowledge in his eyes had her nodding instead. "No."

"Yes," he said simply.

She shook her head, but then said, "Yes," repeating what he'd said.

And that fast, the look of anger in Joshua's eyes was gone, replaced by amusement. He nodded in affirmative, just like she had and said, "No?" and then shook his head, again like she had and said, "Yes?" Then he laughed.

She frowned. "Will you stop that!"

She pulled away and went into the living room where she flopped very dramatically, she thought, down on the sofa.

"Stop what?" he asked, draping the towel around his neck and seating himself.

The dark blue of his dress shirt looked almost black where it was wet. She noted he wore casual slacks and loafers. "Stop laughing. Stop confusing me. Take your pick."

He continued to grin, those deep dimples of his cutting their way up both sides of his face. "Only if you'll stop scaring ten years off my life."

His first words when he entered her apartment came back to her now. "The phone," she said softly.

Joshua sobered. "Yeah. The phone."

Her gaze slid away.

Joshua got up out of the chair and moved across the room to sit down on the sofa, right next to her. "Which brings us full circle. I think it's time you and I talk."

"Which you mentioned earlier," she whispered.

He nodded. "It's time you give me an idea of what's going on, Lilly Hammond. Your life just might depend on it."

Chapter Ten

Joshua studied the woman in front of him. He couldn't begin to tell her the fear that had slid down his spine, wrapping its way around him in cold tendrils of dread when she'd slammed the receiver in his ear—not once but twice.

"You called me?" she asked now.

"Yes, I did." Absently he rubbed his knee.

"Why?" she asked. The soft query, quavering with remorse and fear from something else, colored her question.

He wasn't about to answer her inquiry, however, and get sidetracked.

He wanted his questions answered first.

Reaching out, taking her soft hands, he realized his own rougher ones were slightly chilly. He could smell the scent of soap and discerned from her damp hair that hung around her face in permed ringlets that she'd just gotten out of the shower. "Answer my question, Lilly. Why did you take your phone off the hook?"

Her gaze slid toward the ground and he realized she was trying to think up an excuse. Squeezing her hands to get her attention, he asked, "You've been getting hang-up calls, haven't you?"

It was obvious. Why did most women take the phone off the hook? To either avoid someone they knew, which they could easily do with Caller ID, or to stop the calls completely.

He noted she had no Caller ID and planned to remedy that tomorrow.

Shoulders slumping, Lilly finally nodded.

"Why do they scare you so?" he prodded gently, using his thumbs to rub over the tops of her hands. She shrugged but he'd have none of it.

"Lilly," he commanded softly, his voice demanding she look at him.

Her gaze lifted, meeting his.

"I was in the business for years. I recognize the signs. Someone is stalking you. It's in the way you dress, the way you take your phone off the hook and the fact you didn't acknowledge me at the door until you knew who I was. On that note, I'd like to mention I'm glad you didn't just open your door. Too many women do that these days," he said. "You can't fool me. I am an expert at recognizing certain signs, including when someone is trying to lie to me. So, don't lie now, Lilly. Tell me who is stalking you…and why?"

He saw Lilly swallow, saw the fears crop up in her gaze. "I prayed, asking God for help. I just can't handle this again."

The picture was filling in, like a canvas with only an outline of colors. She was going back and using a fresh stroke to add depth and meaning to those earlier strokes. "Did you ever consider that maybe God sent me to help you?" he asked. He didn't see himself as a hero that God would send to help someone, but he did have experience in the area. And he did know God worked in odd ways sometimes— so maybe he was meant to help her.

He watched as the fear receded and a sort of relief filled her. "I don't want anything to happen to you," she finally said.

His heart swelled at her words. She cared on some level. And so did he, he admitted. Boy, were her hands soft, he thought, as they curled into his larger ones, accepting the comfort as he rubbed his thumbs again and again over the tops of them.

"I'm a big boy, Lilly. I can watch out for myself."

Her gaze skittered to his knee and he admitted then and there, she did have a right to doubt that. He sighed and released her hands.

Turning, he leaned back on the sofa. Taking the towel from around his neck he blotted at his face.

"Several years ago, I had been assigned to protect a woman and her son," he started, realizing he owed her this if he wanted her to put her trust in him. "She'd turned evidence and was a witness and needed protection from some bad people."

Out of his peripheral he saw Lilly listening intently. She leaned toward him slightly, though she probably didn't realize it. Her gaze was open, honest and filled with curiosity and maybe just a bit of concern as she listened.

"I put her and her child in a back room. I knew the bad guys had found where we were, but backup was on the way." He remembered the argument with Carrie about that. She was absolutely terrified that the thugs were going to kill her. No amount of persuasion could convince her he could protect her. Of course, as deeply as he cared for her, he could see Carrie's point of view. She knew he had told her he loved her. Just that night, as a matter of fact. She told him, in no uncertain terms, that she didn't want his love, that love would cause her to end up dead. She had loved him, which was okay, but when he'd finally confessed his love...

"Carrie felt she and Andy would be safer away from the house, from the place I'd told them to say. She knew it would be dangerous and thought... Well, it doesn't matter. What does matter is that I tried to protect them and both of them ended up dead."

What he didn't say was that Carrie had thought she was protecting herself by leaving.

"I'm sorry."

Joshua swiveled his head toward her. "Communication is very important when you're frightened or concerned about something."

She nodded.

He shivered slightly from the wet shirt.

She must have seen it. She stood. "Do you like cocoa? I have cocoa I can make up."

"Haven't you had dinner yet?" he asked. It was nearly 7:00 p.m. Of course, he hadn't had dinner, but that was because he'd been out in Pride when he'd called her and then driven forty-five minutes to get here.

She shrugged. "I hadn't gotten around to it."

"I know this great little place that serves Italian food. Do you feel like dinner out?"

Realizing he'd just asked her on a date, he paused. He hadn't meant to move that fast. One wrong word... He waited, knowing it was too late to take it back. If she said no, then that was it.

Todd's words came back to him and he admitted that, had he not been so freaked over the fact that he hadn't been able to get hold of

Lilly and he was certain something had happened, he most likely wouldn't have asked her out tonight. He did care what people thought and despite his attraction to her, had been avoiding anything too personal. Especially since he knew someone was after her.

He watched her gaze and then finally she nodded. "Okay."

Warmth suffused his body and he smiled. "Go change," he said.

"I'll be just a minute." She turned and hurried out of the room.

It wasn't until he was alone that he realized she'd never answered his questions.

Man, he thought disgustedly, Matt had been right. He had it bad if he was letting it interfere with his objectivity. And that could cause problems down the line.

After all, she admitted there was a stalker.

It was likely the stalker knew who she worked with and would most likely figure out if Lilly had taken her working relationship with Joshua a step forward into a personal relationship.

That didn't bode well, if it was someone

who was possessive of Lilly or someone who felt spurned.

He needed to know what was going on, and soon.

Lilly came out of her room, dressed in a nice set of purple silk pants and an off-white top which she'd probably have some name for like ecru or barely ivory or who knew what else. Women and their colors. Still, it looked nice on her. The blouse had long sleeves and a tie at the neck. It was old-fashioned, but attractive.

He allowed his gaze to show her how much he liked the outfit as he stood. And then, in case she missed that, he added, "Nice."

She blushed.

He walked to the door and, seeing an umbrella of Lilly's, he grabbed it. Pulling the front door open, he jostled his cane so he could snap the umbrella wide. Then he turned to wait for her.

"Don't you have an umbrella?" she asked as she grabbed her purse and keys—forgetting the glasses he noticed—and stepped out under the protection of the umbrella he held.

"I have one. But my mind was on other

things,'' he said dryly as she pulled the door closed and locked it.

Slipping a protective arm around Lilly, holding the cane behind her as he did, he scanned the area for anyone out of place and to familiarize himself with what looked normal. It was hard not to be distracted by the warm tiny frame so close to his own. He worked hard to ignore it and to concentrate as he limped across the parking lot on his bum leg. It was worth it, however, to have his arm around Lilly.

His shirt was almost dry, so, instead of returning to Pride to change, he decided to air dry. With the heater on low to help dry him out, he'd be only a little wrinkled when they arrived at the café.

At the car he opened her door and waited until she was in before going around to his side and sliding in behind the wheel. He propped the cane against the door. His knee was throbbing tonight.

Starting the car, he backed out and started driving. ''Thanks for dinner,'' Lilly started.

Joshua chuckled. ''You'd better hold off on that thanks until after dinner. I still want my answers.''

"Oh."

He could tell she'd thought he had forgotten.

Turning onto the main street in front of her apartment complex he left the area. It was only minutes before they were in the heart of Baton Rouge.

They parked and he came around, holding the umbrella for her. Ever alert, he escorted her inside and followed the waitress as she led them to a darkened area in the restaurant back in a corner, away from prying eyes.

He ate here a lot and the hostess knew where he liked to sit.

Seating Lilly first, he sat down across from her. Accepting the dark-green menus, he nodded.

He knew what he wanted and Lilly evidently did too. It took her only a moment to decide.

After the waitress took their orders, Lilly rested her arms on the table. She tried to look relaxed, but he could tell she was nervous.

"It's time for your story," he said softly.

Reluctantly, she nodded.

He waited.

The waitress returned with their tea, and

Lilly took a sip before starting. "Taylor is the name of the man who is following me."

"Taylor." He sounded it out on his lips, deciding he didn't like the name.

"I knew him before I was a Christian. He seemed nice, and exactly the man I had been searching for. He believed in any type of self-expression, wasn't the least bit condemning and made me feel like I had a family again."

"Again?" he asked when she paused.

"My mom and dad had recently died in an auto accident. I was away at college when it happened. I was studying to get my teaching degree in elementary education, actually. I know it sounds so old-fashioned but all I really wanted to do was teach kids."

"There's nothing the matter with that," Joshua said.

"My mom thought there was. She and Dad both had PhDs in Psychology. My mom's minor was philosophy. Needless to say, my mom felt I was letting the female race down with a major like that. If she could only see what I'm doing now!" She laughed bitterly. Her laughter was tinged with a sad note of regret.

"You miss them?" he asked.

"Despite the fact that we disagreed on schooling and they were always psychoanalyzing me, yeah. I know they loved me. That's why Dad insisted my mom let me get the wildness out of my system by encouraging me to take some classes at college. He figured I'd eventually find something better to major in, once I was there at Oklahoma University."

He nodded.

"They had driven to a conference in Springfield, Missouri, and it was there, on their way back, that they were in the fatal accident."

"You didn't stay in school." He knew that for a fact.

"No. I moved back to Tulsa. My parents had lived there seven years. I made arrangements to sell their house. It was awful. I had to have a yard sale to get rid of things that I didn't want. I had to do all kinds of minor things like running the obituary. And of course, I had to make sure the death-in-the-family yard sale ad got into the paper on time. You see, I had planned to go back to school. I was still in shock and it just seemed natural to try to have everything done by the weekend so I could go back to school by Monday. One and a half weeks out of school didn't seem too much for a death. It was at the yard sale that I met Taylor and a young man who was with him named Tristan.''

Joshua made note of the new name to add to a list. Later when he started checking out everything he would look both names up.

"Taylor was so helpful when he found out my parents had died. He stayed and talked, he counseled me. He was very caring.''

The food arrived. They'd both ordered specials. Joshua bowed his head and said a silent prayer as did Lilly. When she was done, she spread her napkin in her lap and tasted her food. Joshua did, too. As usual, the eggplant Parmesan was well prepared tonight. As Joshua ate, he thought about this Taylor guy. Taylor must have known from the obituary and death-in-the-family yard sale ad that Lilly had lost her parents and would be vulnerable. Taylor had singled Lilly out for a purpose. But what?

She took a bite of her spaghetti and then a sip of tea before continuing. ''I moved in with his friends. But it wasn't long before Taylor and I became intimate and I moved in with him.''

He kept any reaction off his face, even though his curiosity was now in high gear. ''Moved in with his friends?'' he asked as casually as possible.

''Not sex or anything,'' she said and he could tell she was hiding something, the way her eyes darted away. She took another bite of her noodles.

''At any rate, though I later thought sex and living with Taylor was filling my needs, it got to where I felt empty inside. The pain that he had alleviated from my parents' death and the loneliness were gone, but there was still an emptiness. I couldn't explain it. However, one day, while out shopping, I met a young woman at the checkout. She had five kids and a sixth one on the way.''

Joshua winced.

''Well, yeah,'' Lilly said, obviously seeing him wince. ''I asked her how she could deal with so many kids. She laughed and told me God gave her the grace.''

"I don't want that type of grace," Joshua joked.

"I love kids," Lilly said. "I always wanted three or four. Taylor and I had even discussed having one, but, that was before I found out he already had three children by three different women."

Don't judge, Joshua told himself. She had admitted she wasn't a Christian during that period of her life.

"Sometimes I think back to that life and wonder how I didn't end up with AIDS or some other disease."

"The grace of God," Joshua said simply and meant it. It was a miracle, in his opinion.

She nodded. "It still haunts me. I wonder if one day I'll meet a man who can deal with my past, who can accept what happened. I mean, there are days I think back about it and can't even stand myself, remembering how I lived. We didn't see anything wrong with drugs or alcohol if it was used 'the right' way, which meant according to Taylor."

She shook her head.

"This guy is sick," Joshua muttered.

Lilly nodded. "It was all a lie. A great big lie. I still sometimes ask God to take those memories away. They're nightmares now. But then, I realize if I didn't remember the past, I couldn't be so thankful for the now, for what God has given me, for what He gave me that day through that woman who had all of those kids."

"She led you to the Lord?"

Lilly nodded. "She started out into the parking lot and I offered to help her. You see, I thought I had some good information for her about joy and how wonderful life really could be."

"Even though you were feeling empty and lost."

"You know, that is *exactly* what that woman said to me. I had no idea at the time how she knew that, but she did. And then she told me that emptiness was a vacuum that only God could fill. I had to realize that Jesus was the messiah and had come to die for my sins. That Jesus loved me and wanted me to come into His fold."

"Sounds like one smart woman."

"Shc was. I didn't know her. I wish I'd asked. I mean, I only helped her with her groceries and her kids, mentioning how I hoped to teach kids the same age as one of her daughters. I hadn't expected to have a life-changing experience."

Joshua was glad for her. "What happened then?"

"Well, I was excited. I thought Taylor would be thrilled that I had found the real truth. I rushed home to tell him."

"He wasn't happy," Joshua surmised, listening to her story and feeling something was right out of his grasp, but not sure what he was missing. She was dancing around something. Just what, he wasn't sure.

Finishing up his meal he pushed his plate away and leaned back in his chair, crossing his legs.

"He was furious. He insisted it was all wrong and forbade me to talk about it again."

"Your grocery store mom would have loved him," Joshua said sarcastically, hearing that the man had forbade her.

"She would have hated them and what I had

gotten into. Still, though I was upset, I didn't say anything else. But suddenly I wasn't happy there, and I wasn't happy in the same room with Taylor—but I couldn't tell him. And I had a feeling if I tried to leave him, he wouldn't be happy. I noticed he never allowed me to go shopping alone anymore.''

Things snapped into place. Joshua straightened, slowly, working not to distract Lilly from her tale, but he suddenly had an idea what he'd been missing, what she hadn't been telling him.

"If I talked to anyone, Taylor somehow always knew.''

Joshua nodded. "He would.''

If she noticed anything odd about his statement, she didn't say so. Instead, she continued. "It was about two months after this that I finally found a way out. I was continuing to pray every night, though my life with Taylor hadn't changed—outwardly at least. Inwardly, however, I was at war. I knew all of this with him was wrong, but I didn't know how to get out. He was gone for the night—probably with another woman," she said bitterly. "I found out he slept around even while I wasn't allowed to

because I was *his*—not that I wanted to but…''
She shook her head. ''At any rate, I was deep
in prayer and the strangest thing happened. It
was like this wind, ever so gentle, blew in, surrounding me, wrapping me in a warmth I'd
never experienced. The sudden joy I felt, like
nothing I could really explain, engulfed me. I
started crying—finally letting loose and just
telling God everything and then…well…''

Her gaze slid away.

''Go on,'' he encouraged.

''You won't believe me. But well, this man
came in and told me to come with him. I did.
I wasn't scared or anything, you know. I just
figured Taylor wanted me. So, I followed him.
We walked away from Taylor, away from the
life I had known, down into town to a small
mission, square in the middle of the nearby
city. We were a good mile and a half away
from the compound where our commune was
when we came to this place. The man who'd
led me, not speaking except when I tried to
back out, told me to go in there and they could
help me. I walked up to the door, scared and
unsure but knocked. They immediately took
me in without question.''

"What happened to the man who helped you?"

"Someone told me they thought it might be Elijah, a sweet older man who ran the bank. He was a very devout man of God. Seems he lost his daughter to Taylor a couple of years before. It didn't really matter who he was. Obviously God had heard my prayers and sent someone to help me."

He chuckled.

So did she. "To this day I don't know who he was. I guess I'm not good at getting names, am I?" she joked. "I do know when I get to heaven I am finding that person as well as the woman with all of those children and I am going to thank them both for what they did for me."

Joshua nodded. "There are still some good people left out there, it seems," he added, smiling.

"Yeah." She smiled at him, with such a tender smile that he actually became uncomfortable.

"I'm not one of those people, Lilly. I am responsible for the deaths of two people I was supposed to be watching."

"I had to learn, though I still sometimes fall into self-condemnation, that God forgets the past when we ask for forgiveness. According to the pastor of that mission, you can pray all you want about the past, but God is just going to say, 'What are you talking about, child? What's that?' over and over and over because He's forgiven you. It's we who must forgive ourselves most often."

Joshua felt as if he'd been hit by a two-by-four. God spoke to his heart as Lilly said that. That had been Joshua's biggest problem. He had never forgiven himself for the past.

"As far as I'm concerned, Joshua, you're an everyday hero. You took me on when I wasn't the most qualified of the people who applied, then when you got to know me, you tried to help me with my problems. You could have let me go. After all, I was hired as a temporary. You could have found all kinds of reasons to replace me. And then tonight, when you called, instead of shrugging it off, you came rushing over, to the rescue."

Feeling more than a little uncomfortable, Joshua shrugged.

She smiled. "And you even admitted perhaps God had sent you."

He felt the tops of his ears turning red. "Enough. This isn't going to get you out of the rest of the explanation."

The waitress brought the check.

Lilly grinned. "How about you give me a break then and I'll share the rest with you tomorrow over a home-cooked meal?"

It was Saturday. Joshua usually went into the office instead of staying at his house alone. But, with the invitation…

He paid the bill and walked her back out to the car.

Driving her home they chatted quietly about what the rain meant to them while he kept an eye out for Taylor, the lunatic, who was obviously searching for Lilly and had most likely already found her.

"Are you going to tell me his last name?" Joshua asked when he walked Lilly to the door.

Startled at the change in conversation, she blinked. Turning, she faced him, looking up at him with such a look of surprise that he wanted to grin.

Finally she asked, "Tomorrow?"

The look in her eyes, the close proximity...he acted on what he'd wanted to do all night. Leaning down, wrapping the free arm that didn't hold the umbrella around her waist, he captured her lips with his and gave her a tender, gentle, loving kiss.

He felt her startlement before she responded.

When it was over he released her and stepped back, still holding the umbrella. Reaching down, he captured her hand and wrapped it around the handle of her umbrella. "Be careful and I'll see you tomorrow."

Her other hand went to her lips. Tears filled her eyes.

Thinking he had done something wrong, he opened his mouth to apologize. Her smile stopped him. "I will," she whispered and unlocked her door. She slipped into the house.

He turned, set his cane next to his leg and hurried to the car to avoid getting soaked and thought, *Women.* He'd kissed her and she'd cried.

An old nursery rhyme came to mind... making him smile as he drove off, distract-

ing him so much that he didn't notice the car
that was partially hidden around the corner of
the other building across from Lilly's.

...kissed the girls and made them cry...

Chapter Eleven

I saw you, Lilly. You slut!

A cripple? You've sunk low.

You were mine, consecrated to me, for me only. I kept you from the other men—better men than this one you're associating with now. But you're such a useless woman—going for the closest man around.

I had special plans for you and for our off-spring. Do you hear the ripping? That's me, ripping up the picture I carried of you. See it flutter in the rain before it's soaked and knocked to the ground? Just as your pride is going to be knocked to the ground when I humble you.

When the time was right we would have had a child, many children, just like that stupid woman you told me about that turned your head. But you didn't wait. You left. You were set up to have the child, the one my followers waited for.

You ran off.

And now many doubt that you were the one. I can't have that. I can't have them questioning me.

You're coming back.

I've left you alone as long as I can. You've had your fun with the world and flirting with other men.

But this man…it's different. And you're going to pay. You and the man as well. He dared touch what is mine, and he's going to regret it.

I just have to find the right time to put my plan into action.

And as soon as I do, this is going to end.

You're going to come back home—and pay for your mistakes.

Chapter Twelve

"I heard from Angelina yesterday. There was a message waiting for me when I got home."

Todd rubbed his eyes, sleepily taking a swig of the coffee Joshua had made up this morning for the meeting. He lived less than half a mile from Joshua in Pride. During the short drive to Joshua's house he hadn't had time to fully wake up. "What did she say?"

"Got home from where?" Davie asked, setting aside his laptop and getting up to pour himself a cup of coffee. The dark-gray skies shone in through the two miniblinds on either side of the front door, casting the living area in an unusual bleak gray this morning.

"She said," Joshua said, kicking at Todd's foot as he walked by to drop down in a muted-brown upholstered chair near Matt, who was wide-awake and listening intently, "that she was going to be out of touch. She had to fly to a small town to settle some business. She said we shouldn't expect to hear from her for a while."

"I should go down there."

Joshua shook his head at Matt's quiet words. "She doesn't want anyone involved."

"When has that stopped us before?" Todd asked mildly, slowly waking up now that he had some caffeine.

"Yeah," Davie said, sitting back down on the light-tan leather sofa and sipping his coffee. "I mean, when Todd was in trouble two months ago it wasn't like we waited for permission from him to help. And Angelina is a woman—"

Todd burst out laughing. "I'm going to tell her you said that when she returns."

Even Matt grinned. "Last time you made a comment like that, she sent a virus to crash your hard drive."

Davie frowned. "I caught it."

"Not all of it," Todd reminded him. "How many times did her cheeky little sayings about the equality of women pop up on your screen after that?"

Davie scowled. "She shouldn't have messed with my computer like that." Shifting, he shoved at the crocheted afghan, which lay across the back of the sofa and reached again for his computer.

Joshua held up a hand. "In this case," he said, pulling them back to the subject at hand, "I think Angelina can take care of herself. Besides, when she called at the office last week, she said someone down there was helping her out. She does have contacts and as much as we want to protect her, she's trained and well able to take care of herself."

Matt nodded and shifted, adjusting his legs so he could stretch them out. He should know, Joshua thought. Matt had actually trained with her for a while.

"As for where I was last night," Joshua said, tilting his head toward Davie who had asked that question, "I was out on a..." He glanced at Todd.

"You were out on a date with Lilly." Todd filled in Joshua's hesitation with an answer as he sat up in interest, his eyes finally opening and concentrating on something other than being awakened at 7:00 a.m. on a Saturday morning.

"Your secretary?" Davie asked, surprised.

Matt asked, "What did you find out?"

Leave it to Matt to cut to the chase.

Todd, however, interrupted. "Forget that. Let's have all the details."

Davie chuckled.

Joshua simply glared at Todd and said, "Later." He actually had no intention of sharing the details of his intimate encounter with Lilly. Turning his attention toward Matt, he added, "It's like we thought. She's being stalked."

"Did you see the guy?" he asked, his features hardening at what Joshua told him. Matt had been undercover many times for the FBI. One of his cases had dealt with a stalking similar to Lilly's case.

"No. I didn't see any sign of him. So, whether he's actually been by her house yet—"

"He has," Matt said assuredly.

"Most likely," Joshua agreed. "At any rate, he has been making hang-up calls, which means he wants her to know he's found her and has been watching her."

"The question is, has he been to her work yet?" Davie tossed that in.

Joshua nodded. "Exactly. It's most likely that he's followed her and knows where she works. However, we need to find out if he's been inside the building yet."

"I'd wager, if he's already started hang-up calls, that he has," Todd added, all business now.

Joshua tended to agree. "But how many times? Is he there as a temporary employee or a customer? Maybe he simply wandered in off the street to check out the place."

"Not an employee," Davie added. "That'd be too obvious."

"I tend to agree with the boy," Todd said.

Davie sneered at the term *boy,* though he used his young looks often to get things done where a young person might have an advantage. He was actually twenty-seven. "I'm so glad you do, Mr. Ashcroft."

Matt broke up the words the two insisted on exchanging by getting back to the subject. "So, you want us to find out if this is the case?"

Joshua nodded. "Not until Monday. Davie, could you check out security tapes?" At his nod Joshua turned to Todd, "Can you check out gossip since you're so well integrated with all of the secretarial staff there?"

Todd grinned. "My pleasure."

Joshua rolled his eyes. Then to Matt, he said, "You'd be good at spotting something regarding customers. I am planning to make some inquires into the Philadelphia incident and then find out just who this Taylor is."

"The stalker?" Davie asked, adjusting his laptop on his lap and making some notes.

Joshua affirmed it with a nod of his head. "Some sort of cult. She was living with the guy until she got saved and then escaped—with the help of someone from a nearby town. She didn't say where this was, only that a man came to her, led her to a mission and then left her there."

"Interesting," Todd said. He was a Christian as well as Davie. Matt was still vacillating about it. Joshua knew it was because of what he'd seen during his undercover work. He had a really hard time accepting that there was a Christ, with all of the bad he'd experienced.

"This guy has some ulterior motive for her. I'm not sure what it was. However, from hints that Lilly has dropped, I'm not sure she realizes he has plans. It seems Taylor kept her from any of the other people in the commune. She was his and only his. He's obsessed with getting her back. She evidently told this lawyer something in Philadelphia and he killed the lawyer, which leads me to believe he doesn't want anyone touching her."

Todd frowned. "That puts you in a precarious situation, then."

"I'm having dinner at her house tonight." Joshua glanced up at the dark wooden ceiling as he said that knowing he might as well tell them. With the danger he faced with Lilly, it was important they know what was going on.

"Are you sure that's wise?" Davie asked.

"No. Frankly I should probably not go near the woman," Joshua admitted, working to be honest with his friends. "And I plan to tell Lilly just that tonight."

"That you shouldn't go near her?" Matt asked, surprised.

Todd tsked and waved a finger. "It was not your fault that Carrie did what she did. You can't judge Lilly by Carrie."

Both Matt and Davie fell silent as Todd brought up the forbidden subject. They agreed, Joshua could tell, but they weren't about to side with Todd and make Joshua feel as if he were surrounded.

"I still can't risk it. If I'm to protect her, then I can't get involved."

Todd shook his head. "You're already involved."

"Not to the point that I can't pull back."

Matt frowned.

Joshua waved them off with a hand as he stood and went to dump his cool coffee and pour a fresh cup. "Making sure Lilly is okay is the most important thing right now. Once we find this guy and get things settled, then Lilly and I can talk about other things."

"Other things," Todd said and snorted.

Matt stood. "I have football tickets to an LSU game, so if that's all...?"

Joshua nodded. "Unless anyone else has anything."

"Just the weather," Davie said.

Joshua nodded. "We'll be okay with that until Monday, but we're going to be in for a lot of rain. So, let's make sure everything is up and running, in top shape next week. The hurricane is predicted to hit Gulf Shores on Thursday which means we'll probably have to hunker down for two or three days of really heavy rain."

"I'll get Elizabeth notifying everyone of their preventative maintenance Monday," Matt said, referring to his secretary.

"Good. Davie, you get onto the in-house security issue and make sure it's all done."

Turning to Matt, he said, "Have fun."

Matt nodded. "I plan to." He headed out the door.

Davie stood. "I am making a run down to New Orleans today and won't be back until Sunday evening. You have my pager if you need me." Again Joshua nodded.

When Davie was gone, he turned to Todd. "Okay. You've waited until now, so what is it?"

Todd shrugged. "Did you ever wonder why Lilly's trouble is so important that you have all four of us on it instead of turning it over to the local police?"

Joshua scowled. "I'm not going to risk her going to the police and them turning a blind eye to what she says."

"If you went with her, they wouldn't do that," Todd replied.

"There's so little the police can actually do in a situation like this," Joshua said, frustrated. "Besides, the police are way overworked, no matter how good they are."

"And you care for Lilly," Todd added. "Though you may not have admitted it until recently, I had a feeling you noticed her when she first started working for you. You stubbornly ignored it, until it was shoved right in your face."

"Your point?" Joshua asked, seating himself and purposely tipping his cup to sip and act as nonchalant as possible.

"My point is, instead of cutting this woman off completely, go ahead and at least enjoy her company. If you cut Lilly off, she might not tell you anything else. Getting involved is okay. You're a Christian now and know there is a higher authority that is helping you, Josh. Accept that and don't run scared.'' Sighing with exasperation he added, ''This is one of these things you're just blindly going to have to trust me on, Josh.''

Joshua didn't like what Todd said, but Todd was a friend and he admitted he needed his advice. ''I guess this is sorta like the time when we were in that near shoot-out together and you insisted I let you handle it.''

''If you're saying that you knew I was right, you're doing it quite badly.''

Joshua relaxed at Todd's statement and actually smiled. ''Yeah. I was determined to handle it my way, but you were right in the end. I just had to trust you on it.''

Todd nodded. ''Trust me on this. Don't shove Lilly away. Trust your heart on this one. Carrie was never strong. Lilly is.''

He nodded. ''I'll think about it.''

''That's all I can ask—right now,'' Todd said and grinned. Sitting forward he stood and walked across the carpeted floor to the tiny kitchen. Dumping his cup in the sink he rinsed it before returning to the dark wooden living room area. "Well, I'm off, too. Enjoy your date with Lilly."

Joshua stood and walked to the door. Pulling it open he leaned against it and said, "Interesting how not one of you said a thing about me going out last night with Lilly."

Todd shrugged. "The other two are still smarting."

Stepping outside he turned toward Joshua and said, "I won the wager on what night you'd take her out, you see."

Joshua burst out laughing. He should be angry that they'd actually wagered amongst themselves on when he'd go out, but he knew them too well. And had it been one of them, he most likely would have been speculating as well. "Get out," he said instead.

Todd chuckled and walked down the graveled driveway to where his car was parked. Slipping in, he started it and drove off through the tall pine trees to the road.

And as he did, Joshua wondered what he would do without these guys. All four of them had become like the family he didn't have.

All four of them cared about him as much as he cared about them.

And at least three of them right now were waiting to see what happened with Lilly.

Family.

It wasn't whom you were born with necessarily, but those who cared.

Closing the door he admitted he'd like Lilly to get to know these guys as well as he did.

Which made him realize that they were right; his feelings had been engaged longer than he'd realized.

"Well, God, what am I going to do about that?" he asked.

Going back into the living room he pulled out his Bible and sat down to read. Todd was right. God was in control and he had to just sit down, spend time with God and get everything straightened out before his date tonight with Lilly.

Chapter Thirteen

He'd kissed her.

As Lilly finished up frying the last of the chicken, she thought again about last night.

"Ouch!"

Jumping when she was popped by grease, she moved away from the stove. She would have baked it if the oven part of her stove worked, she thought miserably, wondering just when her manager was going to get in and fix it.

However, even that temporary spark of pain and reminder about the broken-down oven couldn't deter her for long from thinking about last night.

He'd kissed her.

Okay, so she was obsessing over one small, tiny, absolutely wonderful kiss.

Turning to mash the potatoes while the last two pieces of chicken finished frying, she forced her mind away from the kiss.

It didn't help. Now all she could think about was the first time she'd seen him. That first day she'd applied for a job and been kicked up to be interviewed by Angelina and then Todd and Davie. Funny, but Matt hadn't interviewed her. It was policy for each one of them to interview the highest secretaries—even the temporary ones.

They had a lot of strange practices there. But she was asked about security by Todd and Davie, skills by Angelina. She thought, most likely, that they relied a lot on instincts.

Then she was passed on to Joshua for the final review. She supposed, had she not met the others' standards, she wouldn't have made it that far.

She'd walked into his office. And there had sat one of the most handsome men she'd ever seen. Of course, she admitted not everyone would like his dark good looks or the distance she saw in his eyes as he talked, but there was something else about him...

He was human. She could tell he was a man who kept his own counsel and didn't expect a close relationship with his secretary by the way he talked to his current secretary.

That reassured her that he wouldn't be pushy or make passes. Actually, she'd felt disappointed. Were she not his secretary, she thought, she'd love to go out with this man.

Then she'd heard him get a call from his church about some activity he was supposed to be helping with.

As they were on their way out, all she could think about was good-looking and a church-goer.

She didn't think she had the job, so she'd gone home and dreamed about the possibilities.

Miracles do happen, because the agency had called her to tell her she'd been hired.

She'd done her best to push her feelings aside and to be exactly what Joshua Staring wanted in a secretary. But each day, her admiration of the man grew.

Oh, he had a temper, triggered mainly by Angelina's antics, but underneath, he was a good man.

She'd fantasized many times that she would pour out her story to him, he'd shrug it off and ask her out on a date. It was romantic, silly thinking for someone as worldly as she was.

Yet it had happened—in part.

She hadn't told him everything, but she'd told him enough to send him running if he didn't want to be involved.

And then he'd kissed her.

She sighed.

Her emotions were already rooted deeply in this man...too deeply.

She didn't think it was possible but then again, with God, she realized, all things were possible.

If only Taylor...

She hated to think about her past.

Finishing the potatoes, she dug out a pretty bowl to dump them in, then sprinkled parsley on the top to add color.

The timer for the toaster sounded and she hurriedly pulled out the garlic bread. She'd gone out and bought a cute little bread basket for them, to which she now, hurriedly, to keep from burning her fingers, tossed them into.

She took the food to the table—all except the chicken—and then returned to finish dishing that up.

A knock sounded on the door.

Gasping, she whirled.

Oh, dear.

"Just a minute," she called out.

Going over to the chair in the living room, she grabbed her silky brown top and slipped it on. Buttoning it up, she tucked it into her pants and then went to the door.

She never cooked with a nice top on, fearing when she fried that it'd get ruined.

Peeking out the peephole she saw it was, indeed, Joshua.

When she opened the door, a bouquet of mixed flowers confronted her.

What a dream come true.

She smiled gently. "Thank you."

Taking them she stepped to the side so he could enter.

His gaze slipped appreciatively over her and

then away. He started past, paused and leaned down, as if he were fighting it, and kissed her.

Curiously she wondered what that had been all about even as she accepted the kiss.

"Something smells delicious."

"I hope you like fried chicken."

He nodded. "I haven't had homemade chicken in years."

She moved into the room and then on into the kitchen. "It's almost done. Make yourself at home. I have cola, tea and water, that's it."

"I'll make us up a couple of teas if you don't mind me in the kitchen," Joshua rumbled from right behind her.

She nearly jumped. She was going to have to get used to this man following her into areas where men had never gone with her. Taylor had never set foot in the kitchen, nor had he followed behind her when she went to get something for him. He had loved her domestic streak and encouraged it.

"That'd be great. The cabinet next to the fridge," she said, indicating where the glasses were.

Pulling out an empty mason jar, since she

had no vases, she filled it with water and then put the flowers into the container.

Joshua laughed. ''I see I'm going to have to get you something else as well.''

She blushed. Instead of facing him as she replied, she turned off the stove and finished dishing up the chicken. ''I don't have much use for vases. I promise I'll remedy that.''

She heard ice and then tea being poured and then Joshua moved out of the kitchen.

''I'll be right there,'' she called.

Taking a deep breath, she let it out slowly. He was always so at ease and confident.

Except for that one dark area in his life— that knee accident.

He always had the cane with him, wherever he went. She'd watched as he'd juggled it and the umbrella last night as he'd tried to be chivalrous and wondered if it bothered him to use it all the time.

She picked up the platter of chicken and walked into the small dining area.

And saw Joshua on hands and knees behind her sofa. ''What in the world are you doing?''

He pushed back and carefully stood, grabbing his cane as he did. As he stood, she saw what he'd been doing.

Gratitude flooded her.

"You needed Caller ID," he said simply.

She blinked back tears. "Thank you. I should have installed one before now. The last one died and I just never did replace it."

He came forward and then rested his cane on the table. Taking the chicken from her, he set it in the empty space she'd left in the middle of the table. "You've done a great job here."

"Thanks."

He pulled a chair out for her.

When she was seated, he sat down next to her. "Mind if we pray?"

She shook her head.

He said the prayer.

When he was done, they started serving up their plates.

The table was only a four seater and Joshua had chosen to sit at a right angle to her. Her knee bumped his and she blushed.

He shook his head. "Don't worry, it's feeling much better today. I did some therapy with it last night."

Curiously she tipped her head. "What type of therapy?"

He smiled as he grabbed a dinner roll. "The stretches I'm *supposed* to do. I usually get too busy and end up skipping them." He sighed. "I always pay for it, too. Plus I have a special handheld massage machine that I use to help loosen up the muscles some."

"I don't guess it's ever going to get better?" Lilly asked, deciding if he'd had problems for this many years, then it was likely it wouldn't.

"I don't think so. Anyone who wants me as a friend is going to have to deal with a very imperfect specimen."

"But you're not imperfect," Lilly argued as she finished dishing up her plate.

"What would you call this?" he asked, dryly.

She smiled. "A badge of honor."

His smile left, the two dimples disappearing as his features turned dark. "I lost people that night, Lilly. If anything, it's a badge of disgrace."

Lilly shook her head. "I was talking with Todd...."

He raised an eyebrow. "Oh, you were?"

She turned bright red; she could feel the heat rushing up her cheeks. She hadn't meant to admit to that. "Well…okay, so I did," she said defensively. "If you want to yell at me for that, do it later. Anyway, I found out the woman took her child and ran because she was afraid. You put yourself between the woman and child and took that bullet. You would have saved the child, too, except for a one in a million route the bullet managed to navigate."

Realizing this wasn't the best dinner conversation, she quickly added, "I'm not saying what happened wasn't a horrible incident to leave scars on your life. All I am saying is that it isn't your fault the woman wouldn't do as she was told by the professional in charge."

"Would you have stayed put, Lilly? There was a hit man on his way, who knew she and her son were in that house. The only person to defend her was me. I'd put her in a back bedroom while I checked out the area. The other man who was supposed to be there had disappeared—he was on the mob's list we later found out—so it was only me to do all the work.

"She knew officers weren't supposed to get emotionally involved, but I'd broken that rule. How could she really trust me?"

"Because you were trained, Joshua. No matter how emotionally involved you were, you had been trained, and if you thought staying in the house was safer than trying to move her somewhere else, the woman should have listened to you."

Joshua picked up his piece of chicken and took a bite. "This is delicious," he said as he swallowed.

She couldn't read on his face how their conversation had affected him. She was sorry if she'd upset him. She hadn't meant to get onto that subject. Unfortunately, she'd never had the best of timing, she thought.

"I used cajun spice," she murmured, "and some bread crumbs."

He nodded. "So, since we've covered my life, how about you finishing up yours?" Joshua asked as he took a bite of the home-made mashed potatoes. Before she could, he murmured, "If I ate like this all the time I'd be as round as my former secretary."

Tension relieved, she laughed.

When the laughter died, he simply waited. Taking a deep breath, she continued her story. "His last name is Matterson," she said.

A huge weight lifted from her at that. "I told the lawyer I worked for his name. He was going to make some inquiries about him. Two days later, he was dead."

"You think Taylor had something to do with that?"

She shuddered. "He was always so nice and concerned. How could he be a murderer?" she asked. "I just can't believe, even if Taylor started the fire that he really meant to kill that lawyer."

She didn't know if Joshua believed her or not. But really, she had trouble believing anyone could do such horrendous things. How could someone she know really be that type of person?

"He had a commune just outside of Tulsa. He was a good man just—misguided."

"Lilly, the man is *stalking* you," Joshua said, exasperated.

Wincing, she nodded. "I know. And it's hard to accept, but maybe he's just sick."

"Definitely," Joshua muttered.

Shoulders slumped, she took a bite of the green beans. They didn't taste very good, she thought. Of course, nothing was going to taste good while she was talking about Taylor.

A hand snaked across the empty space between her and Joshua and wrapped around her wrist. Glancing up, she met his tender gaze. "I'm sorry, Lilly. I'm not making this any easier for you."

His hand infused her with strength, though she doubted he realized it. "It's not easy however you look at it."

He nodded. "What happened to the lawyer isn't going to happen to me."

She accepted that. "He really wanted to have a child with me. He was obsessed with the date. I was on the pill because it was too early. He told me I had to be older for everything to fit right." She shrugged. "As I said, he was odd about that. I guess that's why he felt it was okay to sleep with other women."

Joshua shook his head. "No. He had no morals, Lilly. He was a cult leader. Cult leaders see themselves as the lawmakers and everything revolves around them. That's why he slept with other women. And I'm sure it had nothing to do with you.''

In a way that relieved her. She had always wondered just why he went to other women. Now she was glad he had. At least she could say she hadn't had sex with him that often. ''Thank heavens I never used the drugs he'd allowed his other people to use. He kept the alcohol from me, telling me he didn't want it to make me impure.''

Joshua nodded. ''I'm just glad you're out of his influence now.''

Relieved he had heard everything, she sat back in her chair. ''How did you end up as a Christian? Have you been one very long?''

''Right after Carrie died. Todd led me to the Lord.''

''Really?'' she asked, surprised.

''Yeah. He doesn't talk about it, but that's part of the reason we have a connection. We're believing for Matt and Angelina, too.''

''With two of you praying for them, I'm sure it'll happen.''

He smiled. ''Angelina thinks it's amusing.

Matt just can't believe in this horrible world of violence that God can really exist.''

"They'll come around."

He nodded.

"Have you been watching the weather?'' Lilly asked, changing the subject as she continued to eat.

He smiled. "Yeah. Looks like the rain is going to keep up for the rest of the week.''

"So this is from the hurricane?'' Lilly asked, curious.

He nodded. "Outer bands are circling around. Haven't you noticed we're getting our wind and rain from the east now?''

"It's a huge storm,'' she whispered.

"And it's strong. They upgraded it to a category three just before I came over here. They also said they think it might pick up speed. If that happens, Mississippi is going to be in trouble. We're going to have to hunker down. If it increases its speed, it might actually make landfall by Tuesday.''

"Wow." Lilly finished what was on her plate and pushed it back.

So did Joshua.

Then he turned to Lilly. He had a strange look on his face, one Lilly wasn't sure about. She waited to hear what he was going to say.

It wasn't long in coming. "Before I came over here, I had a talk with the guys. I told them I wasn't going to get involved with you. It was too dangerous, way too iffy, considering what you're going through."

Lilly's heart dropped to her toes. She couldn't put into words the crushing disappointment she felt, all of her hopes and desire for this man falling like broken dreams in puddles around her feet.

"I was wrong, though. It seems I can't help but be involved, because I care for you, Lilly. I care a lot more than I should."

From the absolute depths of misery to the soaring heights of pleasure, her emotions sang. She had forgotten what any high school or college kid knew, dating was a very emotional experience.

She wanted to cry as Joshua admitted such feelings because it now gave her permission to admit that she could easily love this man and spend the rest of her life with him.

"But my past..." she whispered, one of the things that had kept her from admitting how she felt about him for so long.

He shrugged. "It's in the past. God doesn't remember it so should I insult God by bringing it up?"

"But psychologically it will affect me in different things."

He chuckled. "I bet you sound just like your mom, there, don't you, Lilly?"

She reddened, admitting to herself he was right.

"Everything we do affects us and shapes us into what we are. Carrie and Andy's death affected and shaped me."

She saw his hand absently rub his knee and realized that he usually did that when thinking about the past. "However, as a friend once told me, it's how we accept it, through Christ's love and forgiveness that shapes us the most. Lilly, your past is your past. It will always be there, but it doesn't have to rule the present or the future. You can grow, and like you said, instead of worrying over it, thank God for it as you see how far He has brought you from that life."

"You should try that yourself," she replied.

He sighed. "You're right. I need to stop looking backward. I've grieved for the loss, but had it not happened, I'm not sure God could have reached me and brought me out of the despair I felt."

"Todd said she was a Christian."

"I'm going to have to talk with Todd," Joshua murmured.

Lilly shook her head. "He was only trying to help."

"Carrie was," Joshua said, getting back to the subject at hand.

"Then, in a way, they gave their lives to see you saved."

He cocked his head. "Okay, now that is not the way I had ever seen it."

She shrugged. "If you look at it optimistically, you could see it that way."

He smiled. Pushing back from the table he stood and reached for her hand. Pulling her up, he wrapped his arms around her waist.

She went, unsure but glad to see the show of affection.

His next words, however, tilted her world on its axis.

"Lilly, Lilly," he whispered, his gaze direct and honest. "What would I ever do without you?"

As his lips touched hers in a tender kiss of love, she realized she echoed his feelings. What would she ever do without him?

She couldn't imagine because at that very moment, as he held her so confidently in his arms and kissed her, she realized she loved Joshua Staring with all of her heart.

And if she could ever get out of this situation of her past, she just might tell him.

Chapter Fourteen

"It's headed right for the mouth of the Mississippi. We're going to have major problems." Todd's British accent was more pronounced, clipping his words out as he informed Joshua of the latest updates on the television news channel.

Lilly's pen furiously flew across the pad as the bosses held an emergency meeting.

"The speed has increased which means the brunt of the storm, besides flooding New Orleans, is liable to cause major damage in Baton Rouge as well. We'll need to see about contacting temporary workers to help us with all of the repair work as well as get some security guards to make rounds to physically check out the houses.'' Joshua, walking stick in hand, paced to the window to look out before he returned to the conference table, fresh cup of coffee in his hand.

Lilly wiggled her fingers and continued to write. She'd woken up this morning with a note on her door from the manager, rain pounding the pavement and dreams of Joshua on her mind.

She'd had no idea the storm had shifted, or that the rain's increased downpour was any indication that the storm had strengthened.

''With already seven inches of rain, parts of lower Baton Rouge are flooding. We'll need to go ahead and get security out there. Make sure they know they'll get overtime for this.'' Davie typed into his computer.

''We should send out warnings that the people should go ahead and board up their windows,'' Todd suggested.

''And we should see about getting our own windows boarded up,'' Joshua added. Turning to Lilly he said, ''Make sure that is done by today. If personnel has to hire extra people, fine. But we need that done."

"Yes, sir," she said and kept writing.

"Lilly." Joshua's voice came through the suddenly quiet room.

She glanced up.

He was grinning, those dimples cutting deep. "After yesterday, I think it's okay to call me Joshua in front of the guys."

Color ran hot as she felt it rise. She ducked her head trying to cover it, even as Todd said, "Shame on you, lad, for embarrassing her like that. I'd applaud her if she took your stick and cheerfully beat you with it."

"I thought hurricanes couldn't hurt Baton Rouge," Lilly asked to cover her embarrassment.

Matt chuckled—something she rarely heard from him. Then he was back to business. "Actually, Lilly," it was the first time he'd addressed her directly and by her first name since she'd been working there. She was sure there was significance in that. "Hurricanes always pose a threat to wherever they hit when they come inland. The worst threat will be the storm surge, which is the water that is pushed inland before the storm actually makes landfall—or the eye crosses onto land. Therefore, New Orleans, right now, with the incoming tide, is looking at a twenty-foot storm surge at least. They've been evacuating since 6:00 a.m. They weren't expecting any more than ten to twelve inches of rain for the next two or three days. Instead, it looks like they're going to catch the brunt of it. However, because the storm is so huge and moving so fast, it's not going to lose power very quickly. That means we'll still get 140 mile an hour winds up here in Baton Rouge—something we're not used to at all.''

Lilly blinked. ''One hundred and forty miles per hour?''

''Along with approximately seventeen inches of rain,'' Davie said, punching it up on his computer. ''However, though the storm is moving fast and will be strong, it's moving so fast, there will be less rain than with a slower-moving system.''

''So that's good?'' she asked.

Todd said, ''In a way.''

''Shall we get back to work,'' Joshua asked,

"now that Lilly understands just why we're so worried?" He paced over next to her and perched on the arm of the chair where she sat.

She swallowed, but didn't say anything. He made it obvious their relationship had changed.

There was no way he could know she loved him. She hadn't told him yet.

He obviously had decided to show his feelings very openly. He'd been different since she walked in this morning.

She didn't mind, except that Todd seemed vastly amused by his actions.

Lilly actually felt comforted by his possessiveness, yet the haunting fear of Taylor doing something to Joshua still hung over her head.

"Does everyone have down what we need?"

There were affirmations around the table.

"Anyone have anything else to add?"

"Oh," Lilly suddenly said.

She looked up to find Joshua staring down at her in tender amusement. "Another question?"

She shook her head. "The generator."

His smile collapsed. "Angelina's department. And I bet none of the rest of us thought to go ahead and order it without her here.''

Todd shook his head. ''I'll get on it.''

''Lilly typed the paperwork up for me,'' Joshua said. ''I should have seen to it. We'll have to get the extra one from the bunker. I'll do that tonight and bring it back in early.''

''That'll leave you without one at home,'' Davie reminded him.

''I'll crash with one of you,'' Joshua said simply. ''We'll need the generator here just in case this rickety old thing can't hold together.''

''It can't,'' Davie assured him.

''Very well. Then let's go. Thanks, hon,'' Joshua whispered and stood.

She flushed. Standing she hurried to the door and into her office. Rita was just entering with a packet of paperwork. ''Nancy said you needed this for the emergency. Oh, and your brother called. And a generator company called about a new generator you might want to order, though they said it might take three days to deliver it.''

''Thanks, Rita,'' Lilly said and took the files from Rita.

Rita didn't stay to talk, but hurried back out of the office.

"Brother?" Davie asked as he walked out.

She shook her head. "I don't have a brother. It's probably my landlord. There was a note this morning on my door. I left it in my car. He has been wanting to get in and do some repair work and I think he's getting antsy."

"Generator?" Matt asked as he followed right behind Davie.

"In three days."

"Mention it to Joshua when he and Todd get done in there. He might be able to convince them to get it to him earlier. And still, three days would be better than next week."

"Matt?" Lilly asked, causing him to pause.

He turned and waited, his eyes showing respect and a willingness to listen. She realized something had changed with him. She was no longer just a secretary, but part of the group.

That gave her a warm feeling that unfolded inside her and spread outward.

"Is the storm really this dangerous?"

He nodded. "I think Joshua is really upset that it caught him off guard. He hates being caught with his pants down, so to speak. He hadn't expected it to turn. Of course, none of us have. It's been years since we've had a bad hurricane turn and bite us in the rear like this. But this one has done it.''

''Is there anything else I can do?''

Matt paused then nodded. ''Don't let Joshua blame himself for this. Make sure he gets some rest. And be very careful tonight when you drive home. The winds will have picked up by then.''

She nodded.

He turned and strode out of the office, purpose in each step. He really was a nice guy. He was just so…so…empty, she realized was the word she sought.

His life was empty without God.

Sighing, she said a quick prayer for him and then sat down to organize what Rita had given her and start making calls for Joshua.

As she did, she had to wonder what they were up to in the other office.

''Hold my calls, will you, Lilly?'' Joshua said, as if hearing her thoughts as he stuck his head out the door. ''Todd and I need to do some work so I'll be tied up.''

"Okay, Joshua," she replied.

Joshua smiled. "We'll talk later," he promised and then stepped back inside the office, closing the door and closing out the distraction of the woman he had come to love, he suddenly realized.

Frozen there by the door, he accepted that was why he'd made sure all of his people understood Lilly's position this morning.

He cared more than simply wanting to date Lilly Hammond.

He loved her.

"So you've finally figured it out," Todd said from across the room.

Joshua turned, facing his friend and simply wondered what he meant.

"You love her."

He shook his head.

Todd nodded.

Joshua again shook his head. "I can't have that in the way right now. The hurricane, the lunatic somewhere out there who's after her. Do you realize, with all of this going on, I'm not going to be able to keep a close eye on her? *We're* not going to be able to keep a close eye on her," he added. "If that idiot is going to do something, now would be the perfect time."

"I'm more worried about that idiot doing something to you."

"I can protect myself," Joshua said absently.

Todd shook his head. "Not from a sniper hidden in the trees, or a bomb placed in your car. You call this guy an idiot, but I did the checking you asked for. Taylor Matterson is not an idiot. He's a very calculating, dangerous foe. The DEA and AFT have been after him for years but he's managed to evade charges by staying barely legal. They're certain he's into drugs in some major way as well as stockpiling weapons. They just can't prove it." Todd pulled out a report from the stacks in front of him and slid it across the table.

"Thanks. I guess your friends at the agency came through?"

Todd nodded.

"I could have eventually found all of this," Joshua murmured apologetically as he started flipping through and scanning the pages.

"But you were more worried about being with Lilly. So, did you see the guy?"

Joshua shook his head. "I thought I saw someone tailing me last night, but when I made a couple of turns to find out, the guy got spooked and disappeared."

"Did you get a good look at the car?"

"Light color sedan if I had to guess. He stayed pretty far back. I wouldn't have caught it if I hadn't been worried about Lilly."

"Joshua, Matt is…uh here," Lilly added over the intercom as Matt came striding into the office.

"Thanks, Lilly."

He turned as Matt strode to Joshua's desk and grabbed the remote control. "What's up?"

"I was helping Davie go over the lobby feed for the last week and we found something."

Matt sat down and, after flipping on another TV, reached for the computer keyboard on Joshua's desk and started typing.

The feed he was looking for came up on the screen and then Matt zoomed forward to a certain date and time. "There. See that guy?"

Todd and Joshua rose and crossed closer to the desk. A man appeared on the screen; he walked in and up to the receptionist. They watched as he chatted with her.

She was very friendly, laughing, blushing, all signs of an attraction developing as the two talked, then he left.

Tall, charismatic, dark-blond hair and a chiseled jaw, he looked similar to the picture in the file, similar enough to be the same man, more recent than the ten-year-old photo they had of him.

"That's him," Joshua said firmly.

"Looks like it to me," Todd agreed. "And that was over a week ago that he appeared?"

"The first time." Matt tapped some keys and another section of tape was accessed and then started playing.

The man was back, bringing a flower to the receptionist. Matt zoomed in and they could see he was pointing at the register. "Most likely wanting to make an appointment," Matt said.

The receptionist, looking curious, asked something and the man shook his head. She said something again and he finally nodded and then left.

"He didn't get what he wanted but settled for something else it looks like."

"And four days ago…" Matt said as he showed a tape of the man returning and going to the elevator. "Davie is tracing down just who he had an appointment with. We're not sure yet what name he used."

Joshua nodded.

"And this morning…" Matt continued.

Stunned, Joshua watched as the man came into the lobby, chatted with the receptionist and then frowning went over to the lobby phone for inside calls and dialed someone here, in the building. He spoke for a moment, hung up and left. "How long ago was that?"

"An hour, two at the most."

"Want me to do a sweep?" Matt asked.

"Yes. And get down there and inform that receptionist that if he comes back in she is to delay him as long as possible until one of us can get down there."

"I'll see to that," Todd replied.

"The gall that he would come right in here and use the phones."

Todd touched Joshua's sleeve. "Calm down.

Remember, this is normal for psychos like this. You're personally involved, remember?''

The last statement was like a slap in the face. Even with Carrie he hadn't lost it like he was about to now. He'd been running on pure emotion instead of logic.

As he realized that, every bit of emotion drained from him. He could feel the change as he forced, bit by bit, feeling to retreat that might interfere with what he had to do.

"Josh, don't close off like this," Todd said.

"Lilly needs a protector right now, not an emotional boyfriend."

"She needs both," Todd countered.

"Go see to what has to be done and I'll see to things here."

Todd sighed. "I wish—"

However, Joshua had shut himself off. "I won't blow it. Trust me on this."

"I wish I could," Todd said.

He and Matt left to carry out their assignments.

Joshua sat down to prioritize what needed doing. And while he did, he wondered how he was going to tell Lilly what he'd just found out.

He loved her.

And he had to put all of that on hold because the man who was after her was about to make his move.

It had been obvious by the way Matt had come running to tell them what he had discovered. Matt was unflappable in most circumstances. But not this one.

They all understood that this lunatic was confident, certain he was going to get what he wanted—so certain that he felt no qualms about standing in the lobby, on the phone and taking time to pause and smile at the surveillance camera.

Though Lilly thought Taylor couldn't have killed the lawyer, Joshua had no doubt he'd done it, and planned the same for him and Lilly as well. The malevolent smile had told it all.

It was time to make sure Lilly was protected.

As long as she was up here working for him, she'd be okay.

However, tonight, when she went home, he was going to make sure she was with one of his friends. She wouldn't go home alone.

Not now.

He prayed God would give him the wisdom to catch this guy.

Chapter Fifteen

"You on your way home?" Rita asked as Lilly passed the secretarial pool. Rita was just slipping on a long, dark, stylish raincoat.

"Actually, I thought I'd sneak out and get Joshua some dinner. He's still working." Lilly didn't own a raincoat, but did have an umbrella. One day she was going to have to buy herself a raincoat, though it was usually too hot to wear one.

"Joshua?" Rita's eyebrows shot straight up in surprise.

Lilly sighed. The cat was out of the bag now. So intent on all that was going on, she'd forgotten and used Joshua's first name.

"You two are an item?" Rita asked excitedly.

Lilly smiled patiently. If she didn't tell Rita something, the woman would keep questioning her—though that was likely anyway. "I wouldn't say an 'item' exactly." She tried to stall while she thought exactly how to explain the whirlwind relationship between her and Joshua.

Rita squealed. "I'm so happy." She finished buttoning her coat and headed toward the elevators with Lilly.

"You put in long hours," Lilly said mildly, thinking perhaps to change the subject. It worked.

"Maybe I'll catch me one of those men if I do," she said teasingly.

Lilly silently acknowledged what Rita meant. She knew Rita really stayed because she was lonely. Lilly used to do the same thing. However, she was staying now because of Joshua instead of loneliness. "You go home tonight, okay, Rita? And keep an eye on the weather."

Why she cared for this woman, she wasn't

sure, but she really did like her, even if Rita's gossip drove her insane on occasions.

"I sure will."

They entered the elevator and Lilly pushed the button.

In the silence Rita said, softly, "Thanks for caring."

Right there was why she cared so much, Lilly realized. Because Rita had no one else to care.

"You know I do," Lilly returned as the elevator doors opened, letting them out on the ground floor.

Rita smiled, brushing away the tender moment, always uneasy if she opened herself up too much to those around her. Lilly guessed it was because she'd been hurt one too many times. Looking around for something to change the subject to, she suddenly grinned. "I see Kelly! I have got to share what I just learned from you."

Lilly rolled her eyes as, laughing, Rita hurried off toward the other secretary who was just getting ready to leave for the day. Many of them had stayed late, those without kids or husband, to help finish up what they could before going home. Most would not be returning to work for the next three or four days.

Turning right and heading down the hall toward the executive parking, which she also was privileged to park in, she wondered about Rita.

Perhaps gossip was what kept her going, giving her a way to feel connected. Rita was never malicious about it.

Opening her umbrella, Lilly stepped outside, and was nearly blown over by the storm.

Staggering, she caught her balance by grabbing on to the handrail. Cool wet rain hit her as a visible force of nature attempted to shove her aside so it could continue on its way. Shuddering from the chill she braced her feet and then shoved forward. She fought her way toward her car step by step, battling the strong gusts of wind. The overhead security light flickered on and off, aiding her only partially as she tried to avoid the pooling water that gathered in the uneven parking lot.

Now she realized why the little seafood place wasn't delivering tonight. Todd, Matt, Davie and Joshua were all still upstairs—along with a huge number of security guards. They were organizing, assigning and sending out people, handling this crisis personally instead of allowing their department heads to go it alone. Most probably, she thought, it was because it was such a large storm.

Struggling into her car, she realized she was soaked from the short ten-yard walk.

Shaking her hands, she reached for a tissue and dabbed at her face. Even her hair was damp. The winds had to be a good forty-five miles an hour out there with gusts of at least up to seventy-five.

What would it be like later?

The storm was supposed to make landfall tomorrow afternoon and already it was a mess.

Branches dotted the streets and rain was flooding everywhere. They were even under a tornado watch. Joshua had explained the dropping pressure as the storm moved in made it perfect weather for tornadoes as well.

She was learning a lot about hurricanes. Not only did they bring high winds, but also flooding, storm surge and tornadoes were all a part of the package.

Shaking her head, she started the car and backed out of the parking space.

She hoped these guys appreciated her sacrifice. She wouldn't go out in weather like this for anyone else.

"She what?"

Rita blinked at the anger in Mr. Staring's voice.

"She left, Mr. Staring. Just five minutes ago. She headed right out there to her car."

Joshua ran a hand through his hair. Striding over to the chairs where an in-house phone sat, he paused to wave his walking stick at her. "Don't you move."

He dialed a five-digit number and then barked into the phone, "Lilly's gone. I'm going to go find her. Can you handle things from here?" He paused. "Yeah. I'll remind her of that, Todd. I have my cell if you need me." Rita noted his hand go to his side under the casual jacket he wore.

He hung up the phone and returned to Rita's side, walking with purpose, his feet and stick clicking as he crossed the tiled floor. "Rita, this is very important. Did she tell you where she was going?"

Uneasy now, Rita glanced around. She wasn't used to having this man's attention on her, especially not this intense. No one else was around to help her out, or to see what was happening, she realized. Carefully, she answered, "I—I—don't know. I mean—"

"It's important, Rita. She could be in trouble."

Rita gathered her composure. "No. I mean, she was just going to get you dinner. She said you were working really hard." Nervously she continued. "I don't know why she couldn't have sent her brother. He was in town, you see, and wanted to visit her. With the storm and all—"

"What brother?"

Seeing she had information Mr. Staring didn't, she suddenly felt a surge of confidence. "Her brother called today. He just got into town. She was in a meeting with you. She'd forwarded her phones to me since Nancy had so many other phones forwarded to her, you see. And he calls up and said he just arrived and chatted a minute and asked me if he could talk to her. He was really sad when he couldn't. He wanted to surprise her, you see, wanting me to send her out for lunch to a restaurant—"

"She doesn't have a brother, Rita," Joshua

said and muttered something low under his breath.

"But—"

He shook his head. "She's in danger. Go up to Matt's office and tell him just what you told me. I've got to find her."

Rita, the first tendrils of fear snaking up her spine, realized something was going on that she didn't know about, something bad.

Moreover, her only friend was involved. "Yes, sir, Mr. Staring," she said and started toward the elevators, intent on doing exactly what the CEO had said.

"Please, take care of her," she called to her boss.

Joshua paused, and with the oddest look on his face said, "I thought I could do that, Rita. I really did, but now I wonder if it was all a facade."

Turning he sprinted down the hall toward the side door, ignoring the pain in his knee, praying it held up until he could find Lilly.

Chapter Sixteen

Ah, there you are. Right on time. I knew you'd be leaving soon.

Hold on tight, Lilly. I'm cocking my rifle now…cocking it…aiming….

The kick is mild as I watch what happens to you.

Poor Lilly.

It's raining out and now this.

I'm laughing, Lilly, as I head back to my car. I'll be right there. Just give me two minutes and I'll be there to fix everything.

Chapter Seventeen

Lilly had never had a blowout before. The loud bang and the sudden loss of ability to steer, however, gave away the problem.

Gripping the steering wheel she held on as the car went wild.

"Dear God, help!" she cried out in fear as the car tilted as if it were going to roll.

The car righted itself. She bounced violently as it came to a stop just short of the shoulder.

Lilly's heart beating a staccato, she held on for dear life although the car no longer moved. Her breathing rapid, she nearly wept in relief as she realized God had protected her from what could have been a disastrous ending. The car hadn't skidded off the road or flipped into the flooded ditch. Had the car turned sideways or upside down, the five-foot ditch would have most assuredly drowned her.

Instead, she was sitting, almost on the shoulder, the car still intact.

Realizing she could easily be hit if she didn't move her vehicle, she edged it forward until it was well over onto the shoulder, past the solid white line.

Only then did she release the death grip she had on the steering wheel.

Only then did she realize she didn't have Joshua's cell phone with her.

He had called her in earlier today and told her she wasn't to go anywhere without him and that if she got some wild hair to leave her desk to at least take the cell phone. To leave her *desk!* She admired the sweet words and suddenly protective attitude he'd developed. After their kiss last night, she wasn't surprised. Well, okay, she was a little. Of course, she'd felt a bit possessive and needy after that kiss so it was probable he felt the same way. And with the danger that was stalking her, she reasoned that he was actually worried because his emotions had become as entangled as hers.

He'd been kidding, she was sure, not expecting her to leave the building when he'd said that, but Matt had said to take care of him so she'd decided to go ahead and make one quick trip. She'd been certain it would be okay and he wouldn't even miss her.

He was going to kill her when he found out.

Cutting the engine she listened to the pounding of the rain outside. It came down in sheets, sounding like nails being poured out on her roof.

Glancing around Choctaw, she noted there was no traffic. Though Choctaw wasn't usually crowded, there were usually a few cars around. It was the storm, she realized. Most sane people were finding places to batten down the hatches and ride this mess out. People were still coming into town from New Orleans on the main roads, though all of the hotels were already filled.

This wasn't a main road, however, which meant no traffic, *which meant* she could either sit here all night or change her own tire.

As wet as she was going to get, she almost voted for sitting there, except if Joshua realized she was gone, he'd really worry. How had she gotten so serious so fast with a man that protective?

Taking a deep breath, she grabbed her umbrella and scooted out of the car. She didn't have an answer to that question.

Like a chilly wet blanket, the rain enveloped her, soaking the dark-blue, pinstriped suit she wore.

Rushing toward the back of the car, she slipped the key into the trunk and opened it. The wind caught it, nearly ripping it off.

"God, this isn't going to work. What am I going to do?"

As if in answer, she noted a car in the distance, coming her way.

Slamming the trunk, she hurried back to her car and slipped inside the front seat. She'd wait and see who it was. Could it be God answering a prayer, again?

The car pulled up behind her and through the darkness she knew immediately who it was.

She shoved the door back open.

Why him? She'd thought she'd have just a tad bit of time before he discovered her gone.

Jumping out she turned to face the wrath of the three-legged man who limped toward her.

"What are you doing out here?" he demanded, his cane clicking as he came toward her. "You weren't supposed to leave my sight!"

He arrived in front of her, stopping just short, crowding her space as he worked to protect her from the rain. She saw his gaze was, once again, furious, though this time at her. "I thought I made myself clear."

As angry with her as he was, he was still trying to keep her from getting soaked. Despite the chill, she inwardly warmed.

"I was only going to get supper," she argued over the wind, extending the umbrella so it covered both of them.

"You don't understand and now is not the time to explain. Just come with me."

Well, that was certainly short and sweet, she thought, surprised at how abrupt he was.

Headlights from behind her suddenly illuminated Joshua's face. "Watch out!" he cried and grabbed her. With a force not much less than the hurricane force winds, he savagely shoved her toward the ditch, away from her car.

Lilly went flying, losing any balance she'd had. The umbrella was most certainly lost as she threw her hands out expecting to hit the ground. But Joshua didn't allow it, jerking her by the arm so roughly that she cried out in pain, certain her right shoulder had been dislocated. And then they were tumbling down into the rain-filled ditch.

Lilly gasped in shock and immediately regretted it. Her mouth filled with water.

Under she went, lights flashing in and out of her vision as she fought to keep from getting washed away.

Coughing and gagging, she clawed her way up toward the lighted streetlamps, only to see her car coming toward them.

Joshua once again grabbed her and pulled her toward him, barely managing to avoid her car as it crashed into the ditch.

Water gushed toward them in a massive wave, knocking them down and dragging them back toward the vehicle.

Strong arms wrapped around Lilly, pulling her back up against the firm body. ''Come on!'' he ground out over the sound of squealing tires.

He started climbing, or rather clawing, his way up the ditch. Lilly cried out in pain as she tried to keep up with him and hurt her right ankle.

''Come on,'' he demanded, not slowing, not giving her a chance to get her bearings, but demanding she continue moving.

She lost a shoe, trembled from the cold and still choked from the inhaled water, but followed.

Shoving her into the front seat of his own car, he clambered in after her.

She saw the driver's side of his beautiful car was dented, but couldn't figure out what had happened.

He didn't give her time to question either, not that she could as she was still gagging, trying to catch her breath. The keys were still in the engine. Joshua turned them, gunning the engine. Hitting the gas pedal, they jumped into motion, taking off down the road. Lilly hit the back of the seat and automatically reached out to brace herself.

The world around her was still a blur of light, sound and motion, nothing coming clearly within sight as she tried to blink against the stinging of the water that had all but caused her temporary blindness.

Lilly coughed for a good two minutes before her airway was cleared and she could talk. "Wha-what happened?"

As her vision cleared, she saw Joshua checking the rearview mirror. He reached down to his side and muttered under his breath, "I lost the cell phone."

His face was white with pain.

"Joshua?" she asked, her pain forgotten as she studied the nuances of his features.

That is, until reaction finally set in, causing her systems to react in their own way. She reached for him, but instead of a steady, calm hand, she noted it shook as if she had some sort of palsy. Her teeth started chattering, too.

Joshua reached over and gently urged her closer. "Turn the heat up, honey," he said softly.

Reaching out, she tried to, fumbling with the controls. She felt Joshua shaking, too, and realized he'd had just as much of a scare as she had. ''What happened?'' she asked.

''That car tried to kill us.''

''Car?''

His voice was low and short, his words clipped as he said that. Only now did Lilly remember the sudden light that reflected Joshua's face. And a squeal of tires, she thought, vaguely remembering hearing that sound when they were in the ditch.

''A car was there?''

''Yeah,'' he said.

He knew when it hit her. She could tell because as soon as she realized it must have been Taylor, his arm tightened. ''Just stay calm, honey. We'll take care of it.''

She suddenly saw they weren't headed back toward work. ''Where are we going?''

''The bunker,'' he said simply.

''It was Taylor, wasn't it?''

He hesitated.

''Don't lie to me, Joshua. Please. What's going on?''

"Rita said your brother called today wanting to surprise you. He actually wanted you to come down and meet him somewhere. He was going to get Rita to send you on a fake run to get you out of the building." He paused, and then added softly, "Taylor wanted you away from us."

"Taylor," she whispered. Unable to stop herself, she leaned in closer to Joshua, although it meant he could only drive with one hand.

"Yeah. That's what we think. We have pictures on video of him in the lobby this morning."

"Why didn't you tell me?" she demanded, shocked that he'd known this and hadn't shared the important information.

"It wasn't intentional," Joshua said. Sighing, he added, "As you know, I have branches of this company over in Hammond, in New Orleans and Lafayette. All of these officers are on alert, honey. I thought if I kept the explanation about Taylor short and simply told you not to leave, you wouldn't."

"You thought I'd run if you told me the truth," she accused, moving away.

"Lilly…" he drawled.

She pushed over to the other side of the car, wincing as she realized her shoulder which had been jerked out of socket and had gone right back in, was now very painful. Shifting to adjust to where she could tolerate the pain, she replied, "No, that's right, isn't it? You thought I'd react just like Carrie did and not trust you?"

"Let's not talk about this now, okay?" he asked not so patiently.

"I think now is exactly the right time," Lilly argued. "You know what?" she continued. "I love you. Despite all that happened in your past, I love you. See? It doesn't matter to me at all that one of your missions failed, except to see you hurting."

Joshua glanced at her in stunned shock.

"You didn't expect me to fall in love with you, did you? You've been holding a small part of yourself back."

"That's not true, Lilly. I love you."

He sounded so boyish when he said it like that. Had she not been so upset, she would have laughed. Instead, she said, "Well goody,

goody. I'm glad. But you still don't trust me. How could you keep something from me like that and expect me to listen? Why couldn't you have just told me the truth? I'll tell you why. Because you were afraid I'd—"

"Get killed," he finished.

Lilly snapped her mouth shut.

"That's right," he said, low. "I didn't tell you because I thought if I did, you'd panic and run and get killed."

The silence was deafening. He'd been so terrified she'd die that he just couldn't trust her. She sighed, realizing her anger was getting them nowhere. If she tried to look at it logically, she would see that when someone was upset or worried, they might just try to protect their loved one by not sharing information they thought would help protect them. And, she did have to admit that there was some truth to the statement he'd made. His company did have offices in other cities and he was trying to coordinate everything from his main office. He had to make sure these offices and their clients were protected from the storm. Softening, she said, "I'd never run from you, Joshua. If you give me a chance, I'll prove it to you."

She saw he struggled with something as his jaw muscle flexed. Finally, he said, shortly, "She told me she loved me, too, two days before she died. It was all okay, until the situation turned sour. She ended up furious and angry that I loved her, telling me I shouldn't be involved. Those were the last words we shared— before she tried to leave and was killed."

Oh, no, Lilly thought, her heart aching. "But you're my hero, Joshua. How could I stop loving you *or* trusting you under any circumstances?" she said so softly, so achingly tender that she saw Joshua's jaw tighten.

She hadn't realized how long they were in the car until she saw they were entering Pride. Her entire body cried out in pain as she shifted her position.

"I want to believe you, Lilly," Joshua finally said.

"Then do," she replied. "Just accept it. I'd rather die than let you down on this point."

"On this point?" he asked and she saw some of the tension leave his frame.

She nodded. "There will be times I'll let you down, Joshua, but I promise you, here and now, I won't ever break this type of trust."

Joshua swung onto a side street of the small country town and drove almost a half mile before turning onto a gravel driveway.

"So, this is the bunker?" she asked, making out tall pine trees swinging wildly in the wind.

Joshua went around a large branch in the gravel and continued down the road. "Yeah," he said, murmuring low as he concentrated on dodging branches. "We weren't followed, but I'd be willing to bet the monster knows where I live. And it's obvious he's out for blood, so I don't want you leaving my sight. Is that understood?"

"Yes, Joshua." He sounded harsh, but she knew now that his rough voice simply covered his fear.

Stopping in front of the large wood one-story structure, he got out of the car.

Lilly noticed how slowly and painfully he moved and realized he must have hurt himself protecting her.

She forced her own door open, not waiting for him and eased her bruised and battered body from the car.

He came around, slipped an arm around her

and then headed toward the door. "You look like you can barely move," he muttered.

"You don't look any better," she replied.

"Your suit is ruined," he added.

She shrugged and then winced. "I have others."

"You lost your glasses," he commented bluntly.

Unlocking the door, he pushed it open and encouraged her to go on inside.

Seeing he was going to continue to blame himself for how stiff and sore she was, she added her own comment about her glasses to counter him. "I don't really need them."

"I know," he said, slamming the door.

Turning, he punched in a security code. "I'm going to call the guys." He turned and painfully limped across the room and down the hall. He disappeared from sight.

Large and oblong, the room sported two windows. There was a nice leather sofa and a gorgeous braided rug in the living room, along with two matching chairs, two end tables and decorative lamps.

The opposite side of the room, she noted,

glancing to the right, was the dining room, with a hard oak table and chairs. Pictures by C. C. Lockwood dotted the wall, beautiful pictures of swamps. She had a feeling those were originals, too.

The kitchen was separated by a counter and she could see modern appliances.

The hall led straight back. It had four doors leading off it, two on each side. A door at the end of the hall was a closet, if she had to guess, since a vacuum cleaner sat in front of it.

Where the rug didn't cover the floor, Lilly could see a shiny, buffed surface, which meant either someone came in to take care of the floor or Joshua had a buffer stashed somewhere.

Realizing she was making a mess on his floor, she slipped out of her shoes and hurried across the room to where a kitchen towel lay on the counter. She returned and dropped it over the puddle she had made.

Joshua came out of the back bedroom, gray sweats in his hands. "This is the best I can do," he said and handed them to her.

Surprised he'd thought of her, she nodded. "Thank you."

"Bathroom is the second door on the right."

She started that way.

Joshua stopped her by touching her hand.

She turned.

He hesitated then leaned forward and placed a hard kiss on her lips. "Give me time to trust you," he whispered.

"I will," she said and started down the hall, the cold fading as the warmth of his touch filled her heart.

Chapter Eighteen

"Is she okay?"

Joshua heard the concerned tones in Todd's voice. Turning, he stiffly moved to the edge of the bed and sat down where he could slip on fresh socks.

"She's pretty bruised up."

"If only you'd had your cell phone," Matt said. "I'd have driven down there myself and found the son—"

"We're safe," Joshua broke in.

They talked while he dressed.

"We've sent almost everyone out to work and have closed down the rest of the building until further notice. It isn't looking good, Josh,'' Davie added. ''I doubt people are going to be able to come in for at least a week if this thing hits like they're predicting. Remember Hurricane Andrew?''

How could any of them forget Andrew? Telephone and electrical poles had been down everywhere. Huge live oaks had been pulled up from tornadoes and a huge shortage of ice was a common occurrence within a 150-mile radius.

''Yeah. It took nearly four days for us to dig out of here.'' Their building had sustained some minor roof damage. The building next to them, however, had been destroyed. It had been completely rebuilt, though, and was a testament to the endurability of a city after such a storm.

''I'm afraid this generator isn't going to last, though,'' Todd said into the silence.

The generator.

''I'd forgotten.''

''No one's blaming you,'' Todd chided. ''After all, there are other things on your mind.''

Joshua gasped when he stood.

"You okay?" Matt obviously heard the gasp and was the only one who would ask such a thing with the others around.

Joshua nodded, then realizing they couldn't see him added, "Yeah. I wrenched my knee getting Lilly out of the ditch before that maniac could get his car turned back around to come after us."

Silence.

Joshua tucked in his shirt and grabbed his shoes.

"Look," he continued, "I've got the generator loaded on the truck in the garage. Lilly and I will simply bring it back to Baton Rouge."

"You're safer out there," Davie stated.

"True. But then again, maybe not. He most likely knows where I live. We'll bring the generator back and sit the storm out there."

"I've got a better idea," Matt said.

"Oh?" Joshua asked, slipping his shoes on and tying them.

Matt's voice came across the line, hard as nails. "Todd and I will come out there and collect the generator and he can bring it back while I stay behind.''

''I'll stay behind, chap. You can take it back.'' Todd sounded outraged that Matt would suggest he stay behind.

''Hey! What about me?'' Davie protested loudly.

Joshua rolled his eyes. ''While that's a good plan—''

The lights went out leaving Joshua in total darkness.

It also meant the portable phone went out.

Which was proved true as static filled his ear.

Hanging up the phone, he sighed.

''Joshua!''

Lilly's panicked voice echoed in the hall.

He hurried to the door and opened it. And nearly collided with Lilly as she came rushing toward him.

He didn't argue that he'd been dressing and she could have caught him in a compromising situation or that he was too sore to be catching her as she flew at him like that. Instead, he opened his arms and enveloped her in a close hug.

"It's okay. We were bound to lose power sooner or later. One of the trees probably knocked a power line down."

How he loved the feel of her right there, in his arms, not moving.

She didn't move back but continued to hold him. "I just thought—" she whispered. Then she started again. "I wish this were over. I wish we'd met under normal circumstances. I wish this were all just some dream and…"

He set her from him and reached down, covering her lips with his finger. Then he cupped her cheek. Running his thumb over her lips he murmured, "Then we probably would talk about settling down and having a couple of kids, and work at learning all there is to know about each other. But we can't worry about that now. Because things aren't normal. However, as soon as things *are* normal, we *are* going to have a nice long talk about that."

What was it with women and tears?

Her eyes filled again and her mouth trembled.

Man, he thought and then, to keep her from bursting into tears, he leaned down and kissed her.

"I love you," Lilly whispered and released him.

"I love you, too. Now, let me go call those guys and tell them we're on our way into town with the generator. Go to the closet there and get a coat. I'll meet you in the garage. Don't go wandering anywhere else, you understand?" He said it with a gentle smile, reminding her of just how much she'd scared him earlier when she'd left.

"Okay," she whispered.

He released her.

She hurried to the end hall closet, pulled out his black raincoat and then followed his directions to the kitchen side door. "Go there and it has an overhang all the way across the grounds to the garage." His garage wasn't built onto the home, but separate so he'd had an overhang built for just such occasions.

Turning, he went into the living room and picked up the other phone.

No dial tone.

He sighed.

He'd been without a phone for two days last time when Andrew had hit.

Just great.

Walking back into the hallway he went to get another coat and slipped it on. This one was tan and similar to the other one, but a bit larger. He'd bought it after he'd left the FBI. Living in Baton Rouge he'd gained some weight and the other one was just a tad snug in places.

Lilly loved him.

They were going to talk about marriage—as soon as this mess was over.

He slipped back into his bedroom and in the top of his closet, hidden away from prying eyes, he pulled down a strong box and opened it. Pulling out his 9mm Glock, he slipped it to the back waistband of his pants.

He kept the ammo locked up in a cabinet in the garage. He'd grab it when he left.

He also needed to get the gasoline he kept out back and an umbrella. Then he and Lilly could go into town.

Going to the back door, he buttoned up his jacket and opened the umbrella.

Limping outside, he started toward the small shed when suddenly every hair on the back of his neck stood straight up.

He started to turn but it was too late.

Blinding pain exploded in the back of his head.

Everything went dark.

Chapter Nineteen

She heard the side door open. "I'm waiting, just like you asked," she called out, grinning.

It was pitch-black in there and the electric garage door opener didn't work. Having never had a garage door opener, she wasn't sure how to open the door so, when she'd realized she was stuck in the dark, she'd decided to wait and see what Joshua said about her being so obedient. She grinned at that. Obedient. He hadn't expected her to wait in the dark, but she felt like teasing him some.

"If you were waiting like I asked, Wild Lilly, you'd still be back in Tulsa with me."

Wild Lilly, the name Taylor had given her when she'd moved in with him, echoed horribly clear in the pitch-black garage. The name she'd gone by for the entire time she'd lived in that community dredged up awful memories.

Choking fear filled her throat, cutting off her air supply. Dark spots danced in her vision. It couldn't be.

"Come out, come out wherever you are, Wild Lilly," Taylor singsonged.

Joshua should have been there. Where was he? He was supposed to be right behind her.

Lilly crouched down on hands and knees, trying to blend in with the background, hoping his eyes hadn't had time to adjust to the darkness yet. After all, there was an emergency security light on the pole just outside that was still on, so maybe, just maybe, it had blinded him enough that she would be safe until Joshua came for her.

"What? No welcome, Wild Lilly? Come on, sweetheart. I've been following you on and off for the last six months. What's the matter?"

He called to her in his deep persuasive voice, cajoling her as he had once before.

This time it wouldn't work, though. She could see he still stood by the door. She thought about running, trying to make an escape—but this was where she told Joshua she'd be. What if he came looking for her? If she ran, he wouldn't find her.

"Where's Joshua?" she asked.

Taylor immediately zeroed in on her voice and started that way.

As quickly and quietly as she could, she crawled toward the back of the garage, biting her lip as the pain shot through her arm and ankle.

"Dead."

Lilly forced herself not to cry out at his words. Joshua couldn't be dead. She bit down on her lip even harder to keep from whimpering in fear.

"I'm not going to hurt you, Lilly. I just wanted to scare you. The car slid out there on the pavement. I was hoping to take that boyfriend of yours out."

His voice came from the area where she'd just been. He was searching for her, all right. And he'd planned to kill Joshua.

Please, God. Oh, please don't let Joshua be dead!

As quietly as possible, she moved again.

"I need you, Lilly. The entire group of people—we've grown to twenty thousand nationwide. The Internet sure is wonderful for recruitment. Anyway, I need you. It's time for my prophecy to be fulfilled."

Prophecy? Fear skittered down her spine as she realized he was moving toward her.

Gritting her teeth against the pain in her shoulder, she moved off again on hands and knees.

"You aren't going to ask what prophecy? You're not playing fair. Would you rather me call out 'Marco' and you say 'Polo'? But then, we're not in a pool, are we?"

Taylor and his games. He'd loved to play games with her before. Now they simply turned her stomach, congealing in fear with every word he spoke.

Please, God. Please don't let Joshua be dead, she prayed silently. *Please help us.* The words were becoming a litany in her head as she moved quietly away from his voice.

"Very well," Taylor said, on a long loud sigh. "I'd been preaching that one day a woman would come into the commune, one kept from everyone and only for the savior of the group—that's me, Lilly. And she would bear a child to him in the eighth month, which is August, of next year. A child to be our perfect sacrifice who would atone for our sins so we could then go out and conquer the world. I knew I'd find just the right woman by that time. And you were that woman. Those glittering blue sapphire eyes, so like mine, told me so. My mistake was telling everyone that when I thought I had your loyalty."

His voice turned hard. "Then you ran, Lilly."

He grew quiet and she held her breath, listening for any sound.

"I had to tell them this was a test, that you'd return when the time was upon you."

His voice was right at the corner of the car, she realized horribly.

If she moved, he'd hear her. He was only four feet away. Carefully, so as not to make a sound, she lay down on her side and rolled, ever so slowly, under the truck and closed her eyes.

"Then I had to find you. But you didn't make that easy. First with that pansy lawyer you talked to and then in Louisiana. Why would anyone come to this forsaken area of the country?"

His steps sounded loud as he slowly rounded the corner.

She should have left the building when she'd had the chance. The door was now behind him again. He was once again between her and the door. But she'd told Joshua she'd be here…she'd told him she'd wait for him.

It seemed so silly now to have waited, but then, when she'd first heard his voice, she'd expected Joshua any minute and so it had seemed so logical.

"But I found you. Only this time you weren't mourning my loss."

Like she ever was, she thought, disgusted. Had he forgotten she had left him because she had become a Christian?

"This time you had found a man to date. And what a man. He's a cripple, unable to take care of himself, much less the future mother of the savior's child.''

His feet stopped, even with her, and she watched as he turned his left foot toward the truck and then his entire body. ''Your boyfriend has a generator loaded up here. I wonder why?''

And that fast, Taylor Matterson squatted down and, looking right into her eyes, asked, ''Do you know?''

She lost every bit of breath in her, she was so shocked. Her vision tunneled in on him and she found she couldn't have screamed if her life had depended on it.

Taylor grabbed her by her left arm and hauled her out from under the truck.

The pain of her right arm being scraped along the floor caused her voice to return. She let out a soul-wrenching scream.

Taylor backhanded her, sending her reeling.

Black dots filled her vision. He didn't let her fall, but pulled her right back up in front of him. ''That was for all the trouble you caused me.''

Hard glitters of blue ice glared down at her.

The suave persuasive man was gone, replaced by a demon full of ire and hatred. "And this," he said, raising his hand—

The side door crashed open.

She only caught a flash of the man who lunged in, but it was obvious it was Joshua and his face was covered in blood.

He hit Taylor in the back, smashing him into her.

Pain ricocheted through her body and she was jerked off balance as Joshua and Taylor went down in a heap.

"Get out!" Joshua called.

Lilly cried out.

She couldn't leave him.

"Listen to me!" he said.

Flesh met flesh and she realized one of them had hit the other one.

She backed up, not sure what to do.

She couldn't leave him there.

"Don't move."

The female voice and the gun in her back was nearly too much.

"Lilly?"

She recognized the voice.

Another sound of crashing as tools along the walls came crashing down.

"Angelina! Joshua's hurt."

"Get her out of here, Angie!"

She heard a grunt of pain as Joshua was obviously injured. She started forward. Angelina hauled her outside into the rain and near hurricane force winds.

A vehicle was just pulling up with Matt and Todd in it. The look of steely cold professionals stamped on their faces made them look like strangers, she realized, as they started toward the garage.

Manually, Matt jerked open the overhead door and shoved it open. Both ran into the fight.

"What are you doing here?" Lilly asked, hearing the crashing going on.

"What's up?" A male voice from behind them caught her attention.

A man coming from the house, gun in hand, examined Lilly briefly. "I see you found 'em." He had the strongest Australian accent she'd ever heard. Tall, blond and very well built, he almost engulfed Angelina's tall frame.

Angelina nodded briefly. "Todd and Matt are in there."

"Only the one stalker in there?" the man asked.

Angelina looked at Lilly.

Lilly acknowledged an affirmative.

Staring at the man, she wondered if he had brought Angelina home.

He grinned at her. "You can let go of my soon-to-be wife," he said amusedly.

Lilly glanced down and realized her hands were tightly gripping Angelina's left arm. "I'm sorry."

Angelina shook her head. "It's okay."

The sounds stopped in the garage.

She turned her attention to the door.

Matt and Taylor came out—Taylor looking the worse for wear as Matt dragged him by his arm.

Then Todd came out, Joshua's arm draped over his shoulder. One of his eyes was swelling, but that was nothing compared to Taylor. It looked like he was nearly unconscious and that Joshua had beat the pulp out of him.

"I'll call the police," Matt said and continued on to the car with her stalker and Joshua's would-be killer.

Lilly broke loose of Angelina and with a cry of dismay rushed forward, shoving Todd out of the way and wrapping her arms around Joshua. "You're hurt. Oh, heavens, Joshua, you're hurt and all because of me."

He fell heavily against her. "It's this knee," he breathed, pain in every word. "Just the knee. I wrenched it hauling that psychopath up after I'd knocked him unconscious."

"Your knuckles are bruised," she accused when she saw them. His weight becoming too much, she sank to her knees there in the mud and water. The rain pounded them, but neither cared. Wind whipped at her hair, but she simply caught it and shoved it back behind her neck.

She didn't care about the rain, or the people around her. All she cared about was Joshua and his injuries.

He followed her to the ground. Lifting his head, he asked, "Why did you stay in the garage when you found him in there?"

What a stupid question, she thought, and

then she realized, not necessarily. With all of the love she could muster, she said, "Because that's where I told you I'd be."

He groaned.

Leaning forward, cupping her face, he tilted his head and met her lips with a ravishing kiss of pleasure. Then falling against her, he wrapped his arms around her, holding her tight. "I love you so much it hurts."

"I think it's the injuries that hurt, old man," Todd said from behind them.

"What has been going on while I was gone?" Angelina asked.

"What has been going on with you while you were gone, and do we get an introduction?" Todd asked of her.

"My soon-to-be husband," Angelina said blithely.

Joshua groaned. "I'm not as hurt as you think, Lilly, as you can tell by the lack of concern from these guys." It was said with as much amusement as he could muster—considering...

"There's blood on your face."

Lilly was certain she was going to cry. She

ran her hands over his face and head until she found the injury. When he winced, she bit her lip.

"I was so caught up in my issues of trust, dear Lilly, that you nearly had to die to prove to me you could be trusted."

Realizing that little tidbit tormented him more than the small cut she'd just found on his head, she said, "Let's just not put it to the test again."

He leaned down and kissed her again.

"I'm afraid they've been like this all day," Todd said mildly.

"Well, now," Angelina said as they heard sirens in the distance, "that's good, though unusual for Josh. But surely they've been at this a bit longer than a day."

"Not that I've seen."

"Ah, well, therein lies the problem," Angelina said.

"I could stand to be like that," the tall Aussie said, wrapping his arm around Angelina's middle.

"Not now," Angelina admonished, even though she leaned into him and smiled.

Joshua shook his head.

Lilly, realizing all of these people stood around watching them kiss turned suddenly shy. Now that the danger was over, she realized some things were best kept private. But when she tried to pull back, Joshua wouldn't let her. "I love you, Lilly. And now that everything is back to normal—"

"Normal?" the Aussie asked.

"Believe me," Todd said, "this is as normal as our lives get."

"What am I getting myself into?" the Aussie asked of Angelina.

Joshua ignored them, Lilly noted. Seeing the look in his eyes, she forced herself to ignore them, too, and concentrated, instead, solely on Joshua.

"Yes?" she asked.

He smiled. "As I said, everything is as normal as it can be and I told you I had something I wanted to talk to you about when everything was normal."

She nodded. Her insides turned to jelly. Reaching up, she shoved at a wet strand of hair that whipped back into her face. Her shirt was ripped, her pants brown with mud and tattered around the bottom, but she continued to listen, not caring how she looked.

"Come on, Joshua. Get on with it so we can get out of the rain," Todd complained.

Joshua didn't answer. Instead, he cupped Lilly's cheeks one more time and said, "Lilly, when I met you, I thought you were a good secretary, able to take care of things, manage things and fit into my schedule and way of things perfectly. What I didn't realize was how easily *I* fit in with you as well. Over the past few weeks, however, I've come to realize that. I have especially come to see that I can't do without you."

"If you're going to give me a raise," Lilly suddenly said, certain he couldn't be about to say what he was going to in front of all of these witnesses.

Todd burst into laughter. "Hurry, Matt. You have to hear the rest of this!"

Joshua grimaced. "Well, not a raise per se, but transferring you to a different job. Lilly, I want to marry you and settle down and have those kids we talked about."

"Kids? They're talking about kids? What'd I miss?" Matt had just walked up and turned to those around him.

"Long story," Angelina said.

"You're serious?" Lilly asked.

"He's serious," Todd added.

She turned. "Will you guys stay out of this!"

Angelina laughed. "Oh, yeah. She's one of us already, I see. Boy, have I missed a lot."

Todd raised his hands in surrender at Lilly's glare.

She turned back to Joshua. "There's no one I want more than you, if you can deal with my past."

"Can you deal with mine?" he asked.

"What past?" she asked simply.

He smiled. "Yeah, what past?"

Leaning forward he kissed her again.

"Awww," Todd said.

"You'd better call Davie," Matt added. "He's going to hate that he missed this."

"Especially since he won the wager."

"Wager?" Lilly's eyes widened.

Joshua lifted a hand to Matt who hurried

over and helped him up. The police were waiting to talk to them, Lilly realized, along with Angelina and the Australian guy she'd still not been introduced to.

Todd came over and as gently as possible slipped an arm around Lilly and helped her up. "You've been through too much, lass. We need to get you to the hospital and see about that shoulder."

Only then did she realize she was favoring her right arm. "And my ankle." She held it out and it was twice the size it should be. "But after I talk a moment with Joshua—alone," she pleaded.

He nodded. With a wave of the hand he scooped Lilly up.

"Hey," Joshua warned.

Todd snorted. "He's jealous." He winked at her and had Matt follow him to the front porch.

Jealousy felt good, Lilly admitted, smiling at the thought of Joshua not liking Todd holding her.

Todd set Lilly down in a chair. Joshua dropped into a rocker near her and the rest retreated to where the police stood in the spotlighted area so they could start answering questions.

"You've been accepted," he said, softly.

Tears filled her eyes. "I was always accepted, by my heavenly father."

"And you have a real family now," he said, looking out over his friends.

"More than I could ever hope for," she whispered. "But what do I have to offer you?" she asked.

"Fulfillment," he added.

"I don't understand," she stated.

He took her hand. "I lost my family young and went into the FBI. None of us have family, although it looks like Angelina might just— well, anyway," he said putting that aside. "We'll find out about her soon enough. I've had my job to fill that emptiness that was never quite complete. After Todd led me to the Lord and we formed this group to work at Staring Security, I've spent my every waking moment in work. It was my way of healing from the past. But I never did really heal, until I met you. The day I met you, my pain started receding and the first time I kissed you, I realized there was more to life than just the past and the pain.

"I think God was using you to teach me to live again."

"He taught me not to run," she said softly and glanced back at the garage.

"So you won't run from me?" he asked, capturing her hand and kissing it.

She smiled. "I won't run from you."

"Now or forever?"

"Now or forever," she admitted. "After all, how can I run from my own guardian angel sent to me by God?"

He groaned and leaned across the chair for one final kiss and Lilly thought she was the luckiest woman in the world.

Dear Reader,

Living in Louisiana is a wonderful experience, one I have thoroughly enjoyed through the years. As many of you know, I'm originally from Oklahoma. With this series, EVERYDAY HEROES, I wanted to bring you people from the Louisiana area, set in a tiny little town called Pride, not too far from Baton Rouge—yes, it's a real town—and let you enjoy the life and feel of Louisiana. In this one, you get to experience what we got to experience in Hurricane Andrew, in a very mild sense.

I hope you enjoyed Lilly and Joshua's story. I had so much fun writing it. But guess what? We're a long way from done with them. I just want to know what happened with Angelina and then there is Todd...so, keep your fingers crossed and watch for upcoming books. If you want to keep close tabs, you can contact me via e-mail at: Cheryl@cherylwolverton.com or check out my Web site: http://www.CherylWolverton.com or finally my P.O. Box @: P.O. Box 207, Slaughter, LA 70777!

Blessings!

Cheryl

Next Month From Steeple Hill's

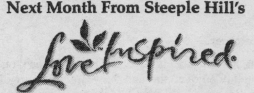

LONG WAY HOME

BY

GENA DALTON

After a serious injury that ended his career as a bull rider, prodigal son Monte McMahan returned to the Rocking M Ranch to make amends with his family and Jo Lena Speirs, the girlfriend he'd abandoned years ago. Just seeing Jo Lena stirred up old emotions and made Monte wonder if it was too late to find love in the arms of the woman he'd once left behind….

Don't miss
LONG WAY HOME
On sale February 2003

Next Month From Steeple Hill's

SONG OF HER HEART
BY
IRENE BRAND

Norah Williamson had spent her entire life caring for her father
and brother, but after their deaths she was left without a purpose.
But when she saw a job listing for a therapeutic riding program,
Norah knew she had to pursue her long-abandoned dreams. And
the owner of the ranch, Mason King, made Norah remember
other forgotten dreams…of love and a family all her own….

Don't miss
SONG OF HER HEART
On sale February 2003

Next Month From Steeple Hill's

Love Inspired

LOVING HEARTS

BY

GAIL GAYMER MARTIN

Esther Downing's old-fashioned father won't give his blessing to her younger sister's marriage until Esther has found a husband of her own, even though this shy librarian is determined to remain single! So when handsome Ian Barry offers to pose as her boyfriend, it seems as if all her problems have been solved—that is, until Esther finds herself falling in love with him....

Don't miss
LOVING HEARTS
On sale February 2003

Visit us at www.steeplehill.com

LILH

HARLEQUIN®

AMERICAN *Romance*®

Celebrate 20 Years
of Home, Heart and Happiness!

Join us for a yearlong anniversary celebration as we
bring you not-to-be-missed miniseries such as:

MILLIONAIRE, MONTANA

A small town wins a huge jackpot in this six-book continuity
(January–June 2003)

THE BABIES OF DOCTORS CIRCLE

Jacqueline Diamond's darling doctor trilogy
(March, May, July 2003)

♛A ROYAL
TWIST

Victoria Chancellor's witty royal duo
(January and February 2003)

And look for your favorite authors throughout the year, including:

Muriel Jensen's JACKPOT BABY (January 2003)

Judy Christenberry's
SAVED BY A TEXAS-SIZED WEDDING (May 2003)

Cathy Gillen Thacker's brand-new
DEVERAUX LEGACY story (June 2003)

Look for more exciting programs throughout the year
as Harlequin American Romance celebrates its 20th Anniversary!

Available at your favorite retail outlet.

 HARLEQUIN®

Makes any time special ®

Take 2 inspirational love stories FREE!

PLUS get a FREE surprise gift!

Mail to Steeple Hill Reader Service™

In U.S.	In Canada
3010 Walden Ave.	P.O. Box 609
P.O. Box 1867	Fort Erie, Ontario
Buffalo, NY 14240-1867	L2A 5X3

YES! Please send me 2 free Love Inspired® novels and my free surprise gift. After receiving them, if I don't wish to receive anymore, I can return the shipping statement marked cancel. If I don't cancel, I will receive 3 brand-new novels every month, before they're available in stores! Bill me at the low price of $3.99 each in the U.S. and $4.49 each in Canada, plus 25¢ shipping and handling and applicable sales tax, if any*. That's the complete price and a saving of over 10% off the cover prices—quite a bargain! I understand that accepting the books and gift places me under no obligation ever to buy any books. I can always return a shipment and cancel at any time. Even if I never buy another book from Steeple Hill, the 2 free books and the surprise gift are mine to keep forever.

103 IDN DNU6
303 IDN DNU7

Name	(PLEASE PRINT)	
Address	Apt. No.	
City	State/Prov.	Zip/Postal Code

INTLI_02   ©1998 Steeple Hill